FIVE'S A CROWD

***Not* For Blondes Only:**

Five's a Crowd

Show Time!

NOT FOR BLONDES ONLY

FIVE'S A CROWD

Betsy Lifton and Karen Lifton

AN
APPLE
PAPERBACK

SCHOLASTIC INC.
New York Toronto London Auckland Sydney

ISBN 0-590-45526-5

Copyright © 1992 by Karen Lifton Healy and Betsy Lifton Hooper. All rights reserved. Published by Scholastic Inc. APPLE PAPERBACKS is a registered trademark of Scholastic Inc.

12 11 10 9 8 7 6 5 4 3 2 1   2 3 4 5 6 7/9

Printed in the U.S.A.   28

First Scholastic printing, August 1992

For Matty, Meggie, and Amy

FIVE'S A CROWD

1

"**H**ey, you guys, hurry! Here he comes now!" Pamela Baldwin was calling us from the living room. "And don't forget the taco dip."

Beth Hanson and I were in Pamela's kitchen that afternoon, gathering the usual supplies for the For Blondes Only TV munch-out. Beth was holding a silver tray that Lucia, the Baldwins' housekeeper, was piling with her homemade cookies and little jelly rolls. I was tearing open a bag of chips to go with the dip.

"Come on, Beth," I said, running toward the kitchen door. "He's on."

"Be right there, Abby," said Beth, who, as usual, was deep in conversation with Lucia.

"Now, you go ahead, child," Lucia said in her soft Southern drawl, adding one last cookie to the tray. "You don't want to miss out on seeing your best beau."

"YOU GUYS!!" Pamela called again.

"COMING!" I called back.

Beth and I hurried through the big arched doors that led to the Baldwins' living room as fast as we could without dropping anything.

"Well, finally," said Pam.

She was sprawled out on the couch. Kate Tucker was sitting on the floor.

"It took you long enough." Pam popped a jelly roll into her mouth.

"Sorry," Beth said. "Lucia was telling me about her husband's exterminating business. Do you have any idea how many roaches can be found in the average kitchen?"

"Oh, please, Beth. I'm eating," said Pam.

"Well, it's interesting," Beth said.

Beth is always collecting interesting facts about Lucia's life. Actually, she's always collecting interesting facts about everybody's lives — the guy at the drugstore, the pizza delivery guy, bus drivers. Complete strangers are always telling her totally personal stuff. I think it's because she's so easy to talk to. I always tell her totally personal stuff myself.

Pam pointed at the TV as we spread the food out on the coffee table.

"What'd we miss?" I asked, plopping down next to Pamela.

"Nothing, yet," she said, reaching for a chip. "This lady is secretly the aunt of the sister of the guy that he supposedly killed."

2

"She's come to confront him," Kate added.

"He is so gorgeous," mumbled Beth through a mouth full of cookie.

"He is beyond gorgeous," Pamela said. "He's a god."

It was a pretty typical For Blondes Only afternoon, sitting around the TV at Pamela's house, stuffing our faces, pretending to do homework, and watching our idol, Denver James, on our favorite soap opera, *Your Life to Lead*. Denver James was the handsomest, most unbelievable guy in the entire world. All of us FBO members were madly in love with him.

"He has the most adorable blue eyes," Kate said. "Don't you think so, Pamela?"

"Too bad there aren't any guys like him around here," said Pamela with a sigh.

The For Blondes Only club was another name for Pamela, Kate, Beth, and me, Abby Wagner. Pam made it up for us when we were about eight, and it just stuck. It made more sense then. In those days we all had very, very blonde hair. We all lived on Honey Hollow Road, in South Meadow, Connecticut, and we spent every single minute together. We'd tell each other secrets, have crushes on the same boys, and eat tons of toffee crunch ice cream. At night, when we were supposed to be asleep, we'd flicker the lights in our windows to send secret messages. I remember our neighbors would smile when we walked by, and tell our parents how cute we looked — four little blonde girls, always together.

But now, we're in sixth grade, and things are a little different. For one thing, I've moved about five blocks away. Kate's hair is more like dirty blonde, and mine has gotten redder. So though our club was called For Blondes Only, it wasn't exactly true. But we still pigged out together on toffee crunch ice cream, and these guys were still my absolute best friends, so I liked to think of us that way. The others did, too.

"Oh, my gosh, she's got a gun!" Kate was shouting.

Sure enough, the aunt of the sister of the guy who Denver supposedly killed was pointing a revolver at Denver's adorable blue eyes.

"Now you'll pay for the death of my beloved Victor," said the aunt.

"I can't look," said Beth, covering her face.

"Oh, Beth," Pamela said. "Don't be a wimp."

Actually, if I had thought the aunt would actually shoot Denver, I probably wouldn't have been able to look, either. But I was pretty certain that nothing was going to happen. For one thing, nothing ever happens on *Your Life to Lead.* The same people have been having the same problems for about a million years. For another thing, Pamela's mother is one of the writers on the show, so if anything was going to happen to Denver, Pamela definitely would have told us. I think.

The camera closed in on the aunt's very crazy-looking eyeballs. Nervously, we all watched to see what would happen next, but then the theme music came up, a Pepsi commercial came on, and we knew we'd have to wait until tomorrow to find out whether or not Denver escapes.

"This is so frustrating," sighed Beth, nibbling on another cookie.

Pamela looked at Beth and sort of chuckled in a very obvious way that meant "I know something you don't know." Then she picked up a copy of *Vogue* magazine from this huge stack of fashion magazines her mother keeps on the coffee table, and started flipping through it. She pretended not to know that we were all waiting for her to say something.

"Uh, Pamela, are you holding out on us?" I asked.

Pamela just smiled and looked for a long time at a picture in *Vogue*. "I wish I had a dress like that," she said.

"Oh, I knew it! Denver's gonna bite it," Beth wailed.

Pamela held out the *Vogue* for me to see. The dress was very short and very tight and very pink. I thought it was kind of cheap-looking, and when I'm a famous fashion designer, which I definitely plan to be some day, I'm never going to make dresses like that. The clothes I like to draw are more old-fashioned, with long skirts and fancy

5

beading and lace. Pamela says it's a waste of time to design old-fashioned clothes since no one wears anything like that anymore, though personally, I don't think she's right. Really great designers start their own trends, and it's possible that people will start wearing long, elegant dresses again if I make them beautiful enough. But Pam likes to think of herself as an expert on stuff, so it doesn't pay to argue with her. That's why I only show her the pictures of my designs of miniskirts or sweaters and leggings. The other stuff is private.

"Don't you think it would look great?" asked Pam, holding the picture of the pink dress up under her chin.

I had to admit, if anyone would look good in it, Pamela would. Not that she needed a sexy pink dress to look good. With her long, wavy, golden hair, huge slate-blue eyes, model-type cheekbones, and long legs, Pamela was one of those incredibly beautiful people who looks perfect no matter what they wear. She even looked good when she was Queen of the Sludge in our science play, and wore a trash bag and a hat with old banana peels hanging off it. On the other hand, no matter what I do, the best I can manage is to look cute. My face is round and freckled, my legs are definitely short, my eyes are greenish, and my nose has a bump in it that I would describe as large, though my mom says she can't even see it. It's hard having a best friend who looks better in sludge than you ever do, even in your coolest outfit, but I try not to let it get me.

"Pam," I said, trying to ignore the magazine, "give us a break here. Does Denver bite it or not?" Pamela can be really annoying the way she makes you beg her to tell you stuff she knows you want to hear.

After about a century, she closed the magazine.

"You don't have to worry about anything," she said. "Denver's got a two-year contract."

I'm not exactly sure what a two-year contract is, and I don't think Beth or Kate know, either, but we all felt relieved when we heard that. I was settling back to do some serious eating, when Kate let out a cry.

"Oh, no," wailed Kate. "Look. I got taco dip all over my hat."

Kate pulled off her baseball cap to show us. It was the official For Blondes Only baseball cap, red with big white letters that said F.B.O. on the rim. Pamela had them made for each of us last Christmas. Last year, in the fifth grade, we all wore them everywhere we went, but it seemed a little babyish to wear them when we started South Meadow Middle School. I still wear mine in the rain, though, and Kate has been wearing hers a lot lately, ever since her parents decided to get divorced. She says the For Blondes Only club is her family now.

7

"I'm such an idiot," Kate said, looking sadly at the red splotch on her cap.

"Oh, give it here, child," said Beth, sounding just exactly like Lucia. "And let me work some magic."

Pam and I laughed, and even Kate almost smiled. Beth can do such great imitations of people. One of her best is of Miss Moritz, our homeroom teacher. It always cracks me up. Beth really wants to be an actress someday. She is planning to win an Academy Award. Pam says it's hard to win one, but I think Beth's got a good chance because she's very, very talented.

"Yeah, Katie," said Pam. "We'll give it to Lucia. She can fix anything."

"I can't believe I ruined my hat," said Kate. "I love that hat."

"I'm sure the stuff'll come out," I assured her.

"I love that hat," Kate said again, shaking her head.

Pam and Beth and I looked at each other. Even though we knew she was being silly, we all felt bad for Kate. She was so sensitive these days. Anything could make her upset. I'm glad that I was still a baby when my father left us to go to California. It's hard to get really sad about something when you aren't old enough to know what's going on.

"Hey, I have an idea, Kate," Pamela said in the gentle kind of voice you'd use to talk to a little kid. "Why don't I French-braid your hair? Then you'll look really pretty when you and your mom go out to dinner tonight."

Kate has very thick, curly dirty blonde hair that falls around her shoulders. She usually wears it loose, and with all that hair, you can barely see her face.

"You guys are going out to dinner?" Beth asked. "Cool. My family hardly ever goes out to dinner."

"Well, my mom says she wants us to spend some time together just having fun. Everything is always so weird around the house now 'cause of, you know. . . ." Kate said.

"Hey, how about we get some of my mother's makeup and do a whole make-over?" Pamela suggested.

"Great idea," Beth said encouragingly. "This'll be fun, Katie."

"Yeah," said Kate, sounding much cheerier.

Playing with Mrs. Baldwin's makeup is one of our favorite things to do at Pamela's house. Her parents are practically never home, so I guess they don't care if we mess around in their room. It's one of the great things about hanging out at Pam's after school. Another is that her dad has one of those TVs that's about the size of a movie screen, and we're allowed to use it, no problem. And, then, of course, there are all those delicious snacks that Lucia makes us.

Even though it's really fun for us, I think it

must be weird for Pamela that her parents are never around. It's not like they're mean, or going through a divorce the way Kate's parents are. It's just that they're incredibly busy. My mom and my stepfather, Paul, can be annoying sometimes, but I'm glad they're home more.

"Hey, hey, look! A Texas Paul's Bar-B-Que commercial," Beth shouted.

"Oh, no," I moaned.

"Yip yip yipee-ii-aay," said Pamela and Beth along with the TV.

"Stop," I said, burying my head under a pillow.

Texas Paul's Bar-B-Que is my stepfather's company. He makes this barbeque sauce that he thinks is the most delicious thing in the entire world, and then he sells it to stores and restaurants. Now that isn't so bad, even though it means our house always smells like barbeque sauce, and all he ever talks about is barbeque sauce, and we have to put barbeque sauce on every single solitary thing we ever eat. The problem is that Paul had this brainstorm idea to start advertising on the local television stations. And the biggest problem is that he does the commercials himself. He puts on a dumb-looking cowboy hat, and this huge, fuzzy moustache that goes down the sides of his mouth, and tries to talk like a cowboy. For some reason, he thinks this will make people buy his sauce. And for some reason, it does.

"Texas Paul's Spicy Bar-B-Que!" screamed Pam

and Beth, with Kate joining in. "It's at home on your range."

"Oh, shut up," I said from beneath my pillow. The rest of the FBO club thinks this is very, very funny. I do not.

"Come on, guys," I begged. "It's so embarrassing."

"Oh, I forgot to tell you, speaking of embarrassing," said Pamela. "Guess who was at the Literary Club meeting today, reading the most embarrassing story you ever heard in your whole life?"

"Who?" we all said practically at once.

"Motormouth Stern," said Pam. "Can you believe it? She's at South Meadow now."

"Oh, no," said Kate.

"I know," said Pam. "Dorfball city."

Motormouth Stern is a girl that Pam and Kate met last summer at camp. Her real name isn't Motormouth, of course. That's just what Pam and Kate called her since she talks so much. I can't quite remember all the reasons they hated her. It mostly had to do with the fact that Motormouth was the head of one color-war team, and Pam was the head of the other, and Motormouth's team won. I think they won because old Motormouth wrote a better team song than Pam did. Something like that. I remember that it really bugged Pam that anybody thought Motormouth was a better writer than she was. Not that Pam is such an unbelievably great writer or anything. It's just that she feels like she knows good writing from bad, because of her mother and all. And I guess she thought that Motormouth's writing was pretty bad.

"What was the story about?" asked Kate. "Was everybody kissing and stuff?"

Supposedly Motormouth's specialty was really gross, mushy writing.

"Everybody was quivering in the moonlight," said Pam.

"Oh, no!" Beth cried.

"Oh, *yes*," said Pam. "So forget Literary Club for me. I mean, if they're just going to sit there and listen to her junk . . ."

"I didn't know you even wanted to be in Literary Club," I said.

"Yeah, well, I don't," said Pam, sounding kind of angry, for some reason. "Now hold still, Kate, or you'll mess up your hair."

"Ouch!" said Kate. "Don't pull."

It was weird how angry Pam got about Motormouth Stern. Watching her tugging at Kate's hair reminded me of how mad she was last summer after color war was over. One time when Pam and I were having a stupid fight about something, and I talked to my mom about it, she told me that Pam was the kind of person who liked to be the best at everything, and that it was very hard for her to admit that maybe someone else could do something better than she could. I could sort of see how that was true in the way she reacted to Motormouth.

"Well, I wouldn't worry about Literary Club too much if I were you," said Beth. "You have too much style for those people, anyway. Look how beautiful you've made Katie."

It was so like Beth to say just the right thing. Pamela smiled and walked around Kate a few times. "She does look good, doesn't she?"

"Let me see," said Kate, running over to look in the mirror.

"Maybe we ought to call up Andy Bigelow, Kate," Pam said with a wink at Beth and me. "Ask him over."

Andy Bigelow is one of the star basketball players in school. We think Kate has a crush on him, though it's pretty funny to picture them together since she's really short and skinny, skinny, skinny.

"Shut up, Pam," Kate said, turning very red.

"Oh, come on, Katie, you can admit it," Pam went on. "We know you think he's cute."

Pamela loves to tease people. She doesn't do it to be mean. She just doesn't think about how upset Kate gets about everything these days, especially since Kate totally idolizes Pam. Even before her parents decided to get divorced, Kate always worried about what Pam thought and what Pam said. Now that she's feeling so insecure all the time, it

13

seems to matter more and more to her. I hate to say it, but before all this stuff with her family, Kate used to be a much more fun person to have around. I understand that it's hard for her, but I miss the old Kate a lot.

"I never said he was cute, and you know it, Pam," Kate said, angrily.

"Okay, okay, sorry. I was only kidding," said Pamela.

Pamela looked at me and shrugged her shoulders with a look that said, "Kate is so sensitive," but I gave her a look back that said, "Be nice."

"Here, Kate, have a cookie," Pamela said gently.

"Hey, Abby, I meant to tell you," Beth said, changing the subject, "I saw this ad for an exhibit of nineteenth-century clothing that's opening at the museum next week."

Beth was the only member of the FBO club who knew about my private dress designs. That's because, as I said before, she's the kind of person you tell everything.

"Oh, yeah?" I said, trying not to sound as unbelievably excited as I was. "That sounds sort of interesting. I bet my mom would take me. You guys want to go?"

"Museums are for dorfs," said Pamela.

Whenever Pamela didn't want to do something, she said it was for dorfs.

"You want to go, Kate?"

"No thanks, Abby," Kate said sadly. "I usually have to spend the weekends with my father now."

"Beth?"

"Actually, I'd like to," Beth said. "But I don't think I'll have the time. Mr. Harper asked me if I wanted to try out for the seventh-grade musical."

"That's fantastic, Beth," I said. "Why didn't you tell us?"

Beth smiled from ear to ear and shrugged, trying to look modest. To be a sixth grader in the seventh-grade musical is about the biggest deal there is.

"Really, Beth, excellent," said Pamela.

"Really," said Kate.

"Yeah, well, I'm super-nervous. I just have to figure out what song to sing for the audition. I was thinking of maybe doing that song 'I Feel Pretty' from *West Side Story*. What do you guys think?"

There was a pause while Kate and Pam and I looked at each other. No one said anything, but I knew what they were thinking. They were thinking that Beth, who is a little bit overweight and wears her messy blonde hair in a hairband pulled straight off her forehead, might look kind of silly singing "I Feel Pretty." I mean, the truth is, I was thinking that myself.

"No good?" Beth asked nervously. I wondered if she knew what we were thinking, too.

15

"I don't know — " Pam started.

"I have an idea," I said, interrupting Pam. "Why don't you sing it for us now, so we can decide?" I thought that was smart. Maybe it would sound great. Beth has an incredibly beautiful voice.

"Right here?" Beth asked.

"Yeah, why not?" Pamela said.

"Go ahead, Beth," said Kate. "I'll turn down the TV."

"Well, all right." Beth took a deep breath and clasped her hands together in front of her.

"Can I make a suggestion, Beth?" Pamela said. "Put your hands at your sides and stand a little bit in profile. Everyone always looks thinner just a little bit in profile."

"Like this?" Beth asked, turning slightly.

"Perfect," said Pamela. "Don't you think she looks better that way?"

"Yes," said Kate.

"Definitely," I said. She did, too. Pam really was good at stuff like that.

Beth smiled.

"My mother taught me that," Pamela went on. "She learned it from working with the actors on the show." Pamela always refers to *Your Life to Lead* as "the show."

"You guys ready?" Beth asked.

"Go for it, Beth," I said.

Closing her eyes and taking a deep breath, Beth

started to sing. Maybe it was because she was standing in profile with her hands at her sides, or maybe it was just because she sang so beautifully, but "I Feel Pretty" suddenly seemed like the most perfect song in the world. I always get this weird feeling of pride whenever I hear Beth sing. It's so great to be friends with someone so talented. I hope people will feel that way about me some day. I leaned my head back on the couch and closed my eyes to listen. When she finished, we all burst into applause.

"Beth Hanson, that was beautiful," I said.

"Bravo," said Pamela.

"You'll definitely get the part," Kate told her. "I know it."

"Oh, you guys," said Beth, with a wave of her hand. But I knew she was really pleased.

"Hey, what time is it?" asked Kate. "I'm supposed to call my mom at five to find out where we're going for dinner."

"Have Chinese," Pam said, passing Kate the phone. "I'm so in the mood for dumplings."

"Mom said something about The Wilford Inn," Kate said, dialing.

"Oooh, fancy," said Pam, raising her eyebrows.

The Wilford Inn is one of those restaurants you only go to for birthdays or parents' anniversaries. I guess Mrs. Tucker wanted to make this a special occasion.

"Yeah, well, it's a big deal," Kate said to us,

her hand over the receiver. She tapped her foot, waiting for her mom to answer the phone. It seemed like a long time, but finally she said, "Hello, Mom? Hi. So what's up?"

There was a long pause.

"But what about dinner?" Kate asked. Her voice had changed from totally excited to totally bummed. "What? What do you mean?"

Kate turned her back to Pam and Beth and me. I sat on the couch and bit my nails, listening.

"Yeah, but I thought you said . . . but, Mom, you promised that we'd . . . yeah, okay . . . I said, okay, what else do you want, Mom? . . . Yeah, well, I don't understand. . . . No, I don't. . . . Just forget it, Mom. Forget it. . . . What? . . . I don't know what I'll do for dinner. I'll just starve, okay? What do you care? . . . Oh, give me a break, Mother. . . . No. . . . No. Good-bye."

Kate hung up the phone with a slam. She didn't turn around. I could see her shoulders shaking a little, as if maybe she was crying.

Pam and Beth and I just looked at each other. We didn't know what to say. It was pretty obvious what had happened, and we all felt really bad.

After a little while, Beth got up and put her arm around Kate. They just stood there together for a few minutes, then Kate shook off Beth's arm and turned to Pam and me.

"Well," she said, trying to sound as if she were completely fine. "What are you gonna do, huh?"

18

She picked up her FBO hat and picked at the taco dip stain.

"I have an idea, Katie," Pamela said. "Why don't you have dinner over here? My parents won't be home until late. It'll just be you and me. We can watch some videos or something."

"Okay, Pam, thanks," Kate said. "Thanks a lot."

It seemed like a pretty good time to leave right then, so Beth and I got our coats and bookbags and headed out the door. I glanced in the window at Kate and Pam as we walked up the street, and they were sitting together on the couch, looking at magazines. Even though they were smiling and stuff, seeing them made me feel lonely.

"I'll race you to the top of the hill," I said to Beth, starting to run. For some reason, I really wanted to hurry home and see my mom.

2

After beating Beth by about a mile, I felt a lot better. We huffed and puffed over to her front steps, where I said good-bye, told her I'd call her later for the history homework, and then headed on toward my new house, about fifteen minutes away.

I hate my new house. I try not to be really obvious about that since my mom and Paul think it's the greatest thing in the world, but if they had only asked me first, I would have told them that the place stinks.

For one thing — and I'm almost too embarrassed to even admit this — the house is on Big Bottom Road. No kidding. Of all the streets with all the names in my town, I have to live on one that describes how I look in a bathing suit.

Now, for Mom and Paul, it's no big deal. I mean, they're already married, so they don't worry about getting dates one day. But I can barely tell my *name* to a boy I like without sounding like a complete jerk — I don't know how I'll ever tell anyone where I live. Moving to this house has seriously ruined any chance at a social life.

The other problem with the new house, of course, is that it's so far away from my friends. Mom said she doesn't think five blocks is really that big a deal, but when you're used to being able to run over to Pamela's for ten minutes even if it's right before bedtime, or stopping by Beth's if you need to talk about something, or even just being around so that Kate can sleep over if things at home are making her crazy, well, then, five blocks is a very, very big deal.

Thinking about all this had put me in kind of a bad mood, so I was already feeling a little grouchy when I turned the corner onto my unmentionable new road, and was practically killed by a girl on a bicycle.

"Hey!" I shouted, landing on the ground with a thud. "What the — "

"Oh, dear. Oh, my goodness. Oh, this is distressing," the girl said as she jumped off her bike to help me up. "It's all my fault. I was daydreaming. Oh, what a calamity. I can't believe I did this. I'm really, really, awfully sorry."

"It's okay," I said, brushing the dirt off my knees. It wasn't really okay, but I could tell that she was going to apologize until Tuesday unless I said something. "Don't worry about it."

"Well, here — at least let me rescue your books

for you," she said. "I'm such a menace. Gosh, I'm sorry. I really am."

The girl started reaching around for my books and papers, which had been thrown all over the road when I fell. She had dark wavy hair, round gray eyes, and very, very long, skinny arms and legs. The way she moved sort of reminded me of a young horse.

"My word," said the bicycle girl, holding up a piece of paper that had sailed under a rosebush. "What's this?"

Oh, shoot, I thought. I had forgotten that I'd stuck a bunch of my private, old-fashioned dress designs inside my math book, and now the bicycle girl was gathering up a whole stack of them. Other than Beth and, sometimes, my mom, I don't like anybody to see that stuff. I held out my hand.

"Here, I'll take that," I said.

The girl ignored me. She was looking through the pages.

"Those are mine," I said, trying to sound very firm.

"You mean you drew these?" said the girl. "My goodness, I'm awed. These are truly magnificent gowns."

"Oh, uh, thanks," I said. I felt kind of uncomfortable. I really wished the girl would give me back my stuff. Still, no one had ever called my dresses "magnificent" before. They hadn't called them "gowns," either, but it sounded okay to me.

"This one is exquisite," said the girl, holding up a drawing of a forest-green taffeta dress with a huge hoop skirt. "A dress for a princess to wear dancing in the moonlight. Oh, and look at this."

She held up a sketch of a black cape lined in red satin. "A cloak of mystery. A murderer's disguise." She looked at me over the pictures and wiggled her eyebrows up and down the way bad guys do in cartoons. I laughed.

"And, this," she said, holding up a drawing of a lemon-yellow skirt decorated with little white ribbons, "is what the Countess wears as she rides in her golden coach to meet with her secret lover."

"What about this one?" I asked, forgetting that these were personal, and pulling out my favorite: a drawing of a long, deep-blue velvet dress, trimmed in pearls and lace.

"Oh," said the girl, putting her hand over her heart. "That takes my breath away. Only the fairest maiden in the kingdom can wear that one. Though she'll look so splendid in it that everyone else will be jealous, and the evil queen will probably send the guards to arrest her and take her to the tower."

"Oh, dear," I said.

"Don't worry," said the girl. "Her noble knight will rescue her. You'll have to draw something for him to wear, though."

I grabbed a pencil and drew a suit of armor with a big coat of arms on the front.

"Perfect," said the girl. "Our fair maiden is saved. You know, you're very talented." She smiled at me. She had a particularly nice smile. "I'm a writer. But I greatly respect fine artists like yourself."

"Thank you," I said. "I'm sure you're a really good writer."

I didn't just say that to be nice. I could sort of tell by the stuff she made up about my pictures that she was "very talented" herself.

"To be a good writer is extremely difficult," the girl said. "But I do hope one day to master my craft. Last year I was a poetess. This year, I'm a novelist. But my themes are the same."

I nodded, even though I wasn't completely sure what that meant.

"Eternal love," the girl went on. "I mean, that's what life's all about, isn't it?"

I hadn't ever really considered what life was all about, but eternal love sounded pretty good to me. By now the girl and I were walking down the street together, the girl pushing her bike.

"Lord Ivo, who is my hero, says that without eternal love, life is nothing but an empty cup. And he should know. He's had eternal love with all the ladies of the court."

The girl stopped talking long enough to fish into the basket on her handlebars and pull out a paperback book. On the cover was a lady in a beautiful pink dress who was lying in the arms of a man wearing tights and a green cape. It was called *Antonia of the Night*.

"This is Lord Ivo," she said, pointing at the man in the tights. "He's just saved Antonia from the one-eyed pirate who kidnapped her and held her captive on a deserted island cliff. It was quite a struggle, and Lord Ivo received a near mortal wound. But, ultimately, the pirate fell to a gruesome death, pierced through the heart by the jagged rocks below." The girl hugged the book to her chest. "I know a lot of people make fun of romance novels," she said. "But those people just don't have any depth."

She held the book out to me. "Would you like to borrow this? I've already read it five times. You might be inspired by Antonia to design more of your extraordinary frocks. And I would be honored if you would show them to me sometime."

"Why, sure, I'll show them to you," I said.

And I meant it, too. Even though the girl was definitely odd, it was cool to find someone who actually appreciated the same stuff I did. And, anyway, I sort of liked her. Sometimes it's nice to be different. Everybody I know is pretty much the same.

"Maybe you could come over sometime," I said with a nod toward my house. "I live right over there."

"Yes, I know," said the girl. "You're Abigail Wagner. My mother told me you just moved in. Abigail is such a beautiful name."

Under ordinary circumstances I probably would have said that everybody calls me Abby, but for some reason I didn't mind that this girl called me Abigail. The way she said it made it sound special.

"I'm Sarah Stern," said the girl. "I live right over there. We're neighbors." She smiled her nice smile again.

Suddenly I had a brainstorm.

"Sarah," I said, "there's supposed to be this nineteenth-century costume exhibit opening at the museum this weekend. Would you like to go on Saturday?"

I wasn't usually into asking total strangers to do stuff with me, but there was something about Sarah that I just liked right away. Besides, if the FBO club couldn't come, it would be more fun to go with Sarah than to go alone.

"Oh, the nineteenth is my absolute favorite century," Sarah said enthusiastically. "I would love to."

"Great," I said. "Why don't you come over to my house at about ten-fifteen and we'll go from there?"

"Splendid," said Sarah, stopping in front of a pretty white house a few doors down from mine. "Well, here we are at my humble abode. Thanks

26

for letting me see your drawings. I really loved them."

Sarah turned to walk into her house, and then looked back at me, smiling. "You know, Abigail," she said with a wink. "I'm glad I ran into you."

"Bye, Sarah," I said, laughing.

I walked the rest of the way home. When I got to my house, my half-brother Michael was riding his bike up and down in front.

"Hey, Abby, watch me do a wheelie," he shouted, and then pulled his bike up so that the front wheel came off the ground.

"That's good, Michael," I said, being careful to stay out of his way.

If I have to be stuck with a nine-year-old brother, I'm glad it's Michael. I mean, he's annoying and obnoxious sometimes, but he's basically an okay kid. At least he's not a spoiled brat like Kate's sister, or a tattletale like Beth's.

"What's for dinner?" I asked, though I was pretty sure of the answer.

"Chicken 'n' sauce," said Michael, riding in circles around me. "Yum yum."

"Chicken 'n' sauce" means chicken with heaps of Texas Paul's slathered on top of it. The night before, we'd had beans 'n' sauce. The next night we'd probably have meat loaf 'n' sauce. Sometimes we even have spaghetti 'n' sauce. Paul believes in being your own best customer. I have a vague memory of eating like a normal person before Paul became the Bar-B-Que King, but that was a long time ago, so I might be wrong.

"Mom!" I called as I walked in the door. "Hey, Mom, I'm home!"

"In the kitchen, honey."

The kitchen in our new house is one of the biggest kitchens I've ever seen. It's even bigger than Pamela's, and it's the main reason Mom and Paul decided to buy the house. This way, Paul can test all his barbeque sauce right here at home.

Mom was standing at the sink, cleaning the chicken. She looked up with a smile when I came in, and brushed her hair out of her face. I think my mom is very pretty for a mom. She's tall and thin and has reddish-blonde hair that is very curly and soft. My hair is stick straight and I can't get it to do anything except sort of hang loose. I always wish I had gotten Mom's hair.

"How was your day, hon?" she asked, putting the chicken in a big dish.

"Okay," I said, pouring a glass of juice and plopping myself down at the big wooden table. "Except that I got run over by a bicycle."

This no longer seemed like the most important thing in my meeting with Sarah, but I knew it would get the biggest reaction.

"Oh, dear," said Mom. She looked at me closely to make sure I was okay, I guess, and then turned to her cookbook. I don't know why she needs to look at a cookbook. She substitutes sauce for practically every ingredient, anyway.

"By a girl who lives down the street. Sarah Stern."

"Oh, yes. I just met her mother the other day. Very nice lady. What did you think of Sarah?" Mom picked up a jar of Texas Paul's and started pouring it onto the chicken she'd been cleaning. Then she pulled out a bowl of broccoli from the refrigerator, and poured it on that, too. It amazes me sometimes how many new things Mom can think up to pour sauce on.

"She seemed nice, too," I said.

"Well, how do you like that," Mom said. "A friend on your new block already." She ruffled my hair. "I told you it wouldn't be so hard. Why don't you invite her over this weekend?"

Mom is always suggesting that I invite new people over. She thinks that the FBO club is a little too cliquey. I've tried to explain to her that if you belong to a club, it's because you want to hang out with them, but she doesn't really get it. I figured she'd be totally thrilled to hear that I had invited Sarah to go to the museum with me.

"Actually," I said, reaching for a carrot stick. "I already — "

"And ask Kate and Pamela over, too," Mom went on. "Since they already know her."

I stopped in mid-chew.

"Who do Kate and Pamela know?" I asked.

"Sarah Stern," Mom said, turning on the stove. "Didn't they go to Camp Woodlands? Sarah's mother mentioned that Sarah went there, too."

I felt like I was going to be sick. Was it possible? Could funny, nice Sarah Stern be the same person as horrible, dorfball Motormouth Stern?

"Oh, no, what have I done?" I said.

"What's that, dear?" Mom asked, her head practically in the oven.

I was about to plunge the rest of the carrot stick through my heart when I heard the loud clomp of Paul's enormous feet come inside the kitchen door.

"Hey, hey, hey, Aber-cadaber," said Paul, leaning his huge self over to give me a kiss. "Just the person I wanted to see."

Paul is the tallest man in our entire town. He probably should have been a basketball player instead of the king of barbeque sauce. He's always banging his head on chandeliers and awnings. Mom has to stand on her tiptoes just to kiss him on the chin.

"Hi, Paul," I said glumly.

"I want you to taste something that will positutely knock your socks off."

Paul always says "positutely," which is a combination of absolutely and positively. He makes up a lot of funny words, like calling me Abercadaber, and saying something is beautissimus when he thinks it's pretty. He takes a little getting used to, but, basically, he's a cool guy.

"Oh, not now," I said.

"But I need your expert opinion," Paul said, tying a napkin around my eyes as a blindfold.

"Paul, please," I said. "I'm not in the mood."

"Not in the mood?" said Paul. "Abers. Where's that Texas Paul's spirit? Now, take a taste of this."

Since it was pretty clear that Paul was going to make me taste this, one way or the other, I opened my mouth. Not that I was expecting a big surprise. I figured that I would soon be swallowing yet another mouthful of Texas Paul's. Maybe this would be the smoked flavor or the hickory flavor or the mesquite flavor, but to me it all tasted pretty much the same. I couldn't help but smile, though. Paul is always so enthusiastic.

"Okay, open wide," Paul said, sliding a spoon into my mouth.

"Wow, what's this?" I asked, pulling off the blindfold.

"You like it? You like it?" Paul was jumping around like a puppy.

"Yeah, actually, I do." I had to admit the stuff tasted good, even in my state of deep depression. It tasted different, somehow.

"It's my new flavor, Jamaican Spice," Paul said proudly. "Delectable, isn't it?" He was so happy, his face had turned red.

"It really is good, dear," Mom said, giving Paul a loving pat. "Now call Michael for me, please. Dinner is almost ready."

It was sort of hard for me to eat dinner, considering that my stomach was in total knots. All I could think about was what Pamela and Kate would say when they found out I had invited Motormouth Stern to go with me to the museum. Even though it was chicken 'n' sauce, which is actually one of the better sauce dishes, I pretty much just mushed the food around on my plate. I'm lucky, because my parents aren't really strict about eating or anything, and nobody bothered me at dinner, they just let me sit. Mom told a funny story about losing her car keys, and Paul kept talking with this terrible Caribbean accent that made Michael laugh so hard, he practically choked. But after dinner, when Mom and I were alone together doing the dishes, she asked me if there was anything the matter.

"Well, sort of, yeah," I said. And then I told Mom what had happened with Sarah, and how she'd turned out to be Motormouth, and how now I was probably going to be banned for life from the FBO club unless I broke off my date with her.

Mom listened quietly to the whole story.

"You know, Abby," she said, when I had finished, "all of my friends thought Paul was a little odd when I first met him."

Well, Mom, he *is* a little odd, I thought to myself, but I knew better than to say it.

"And when I told people that I loved him, and that we were going to get married, they told me I was crazy. I wasn't sure if they would ever talk to me again." Mom brushed a piece of hair out of her eyes.

"I'm not getting married to Sarah, Mom," I said. I knew that was smart-alecky, but I wasn't in the mood for her story, and I knew what she was getting at.

"I hope not, dear. You're still a little young," Mom said with a smile. "You understand what I'm trying to say, though, don't you?"

"Yeah," I said. And I did. She was saying that you shouldn't listen to other people; you should think for yourself. And I knew she was right, too.

There was only one problem. Pamela and Kate were not going to see it that way.

3

I was sitting in homeroom the next morning worrying about Sarah Stern when Pamela came flying into the room.

"Guess what, guess what, guess what!" she said.

I could tell she was really excited because her hair was all tangled from the wind. Usually she stops in the girls' room on the way to class to make sure it looks perfect.

"What?" Beth and I said at the same time.

"What?" Kate said, sort of sadly. Kate was very upset that morning, but she wouldn't tell us why. Pamela told me that Kate had told her that her dad was going to take her mom to court. He wants Kate and her sister to live with him after the divorce. I think it stinks, making them choose between their mom and dad like that.

"I'm going to meet HIM!" Pamela said.

"HIM?" I asked.

"Denver James!" Pamela said. "I'm meeting my

34

mother on the set tonight, and she said she would introduce me to HIM!"

"On the set" means where they film *Your Life to Lead*. Sometimes Pamela's father drives her down to New York City and they meet her mother after work at the soap opera. Then they go out to a real fancy restaurant. The only time I've ever gone to a real fancy New York restaurant was last year on Pamela's birthday when she took the For Blondes Only club out for dinner and a Broadway show. My mom and Paul never take me anywhere that doesn't serve Texas Paul's.

"Ooooooh!" said Beth. "I can't stand it! You're so lucky!"

"Wow, that's fantastic, Pam!" I said.

"Could you get us his autograph?" Beth asked.

"Beth, that is so childish," Pam said. "I would never do anything so embarrassing."

"Oh," said Beth. I could see she was really disappointed.

"Pam, don't be mean," I told her. "You *have* to get his autograph. Famous people's autographs are worth a lot of money. Anyway, I read in this magazine that there's nothing an actor likes more than to have someone ask for his autograph."

"Please, Pam?" Beth added.

"Okay," said Pam, "but just because I love you guys. I love everyone today." She sort of floated down into her seat.

I noticed that Kate hadn't said anything at all.

Usually when something great happens to an FBO club member, Kate does this tap dance that her father taught her. She's a pretty lousy tap dancer, but we don't mind.

"Katie, this is such great news, isn't it?" I asked.

"Yes," Kate said. "It's great, Pam."

She didn't feel too much like dancing, I guess.

Just then Miss Moritz walked into the room, and we had to stop talking. This year is the first year that the FBO club is all together in homeroom. When we first found out, we were totally excited about it, but then it turned out that our teacher was Miss Moritz, the meanest teacher in the whole school. She never lets you say one single thing in class, and she has a million rules, and she gives homework over the weekend. We all hate her. Pam and I decided we should have some kind of code so that we could talk to each other in class, so we worked out a system where we tap our pencils.

"Tap . . . tap tap," tapped Pam. That meant, "Let's meet for lunch today." We meet for lunch every day, actually, but Pam always likes to use the code anyway. It makes her feel like she's getting back at old Moritz.

"Taptaptaptaptaptaptaptaptaptap," tapped Beth. That wasn't in our code, but it was pretty easy to guess it meant, "Aren't you too excited to even breathe!"

Kate and I both tapped twice for "Yes." I was pretty excited, I have to admit. I couldn't wait to get to lunch so we could talk more.

The reason we couldn't talk until lunch is that on Friday mornings we always go down to the school auditorium for a big assembly, and Miss Moritz never lets you say a word the whole time. You have to walk in "a dignified manner" and once you're there, she watches you like a hawk. Josh Baron once got a demerit for sneezing. I swear. So we knew there was no way I could talk to Pamela until lunchtime.

That day's assembly was about Mr. Mac-Fadden's summer trip to Greece and Rome. Mr. MacFadden is our favorite teacher. He teaches English, and is almost as good-looking as Denver James, except he's older, of course. He's very tall, and he has reddish-brown hair and blue eyes, and he always wears these coats with patches on the elbows. He's also very nice, and has a big party for his classes at the end of the year. He spent the summer in Greece and Rome, so he had a lot of slides of all the ruins and statues and everything. I actually thought it was pretty interesting and beautiful, but Pamela kept kicking me and yawning, just big enough for us to see but not Miss Moritz.

After he spoke, Miss Moritz got up and made an announcement about the Thanksgiving Dance.

The elections for the dance committee would be in two weeks.

"Abby, you should run," Pam whispered, since Miss Moritz was at the front of the room and couldn't hear.

"Me?" I whispered back.

"Yeah, you'd be great with the decorations, and I could help you with the music."

I'd never run for anything before, but it sounded sort of fun. I didn't have time to talk about it after that, though, because the assembly was over, and we all wanted to hear about Denver James.

"What are you going to wear?" Kate asked.

"What are you going to say?" I asked.

"Do you think he'll shake your hand?" asked Beth. "I can't believe it. You're going to touch him!!" She pretended to faint into my arms.

"Maybe he'll even kiss her," I added. Beth almost fainted for real when she heard that.

"I think we should celebrate!" said Beth. "Let's meet after school at Cone Heaven and get Blondie Specials."

A Blondie Special is a scoop of toffee crunch ice cream on a blondie (you know, those things that are like brownies, but they're vanilla) topped with caramel sauce. Besides taco dip, they're the favorite FBO treat — not just for their name, but also 'cause they're incredibly delicious. Beth always says that she's on a diet, but it's always *her* idea to get Blondie Specials. I didn't blame her, though, once I saw what they were serving for lunch in the cafeteria.

"Ugh, Mystery Meat," I said.

"And those baked beans that look like puke," Pam said.

"You are *sooo* gross, Pamela Baldwin." Now I had no appetite for lunch.

"Well, I'll be ready for a Blondie Special after *this* lunch," Beth said as we sat down at our usual table. It's right by the water fountain, where all the cutest boys always hang out. We can watch them, but they can't see us, since the table is behind a pillar. Pamela found it for us.

"Me, too!" I said.

Kate didn't say anything. Usually she can put away two Blondie Specials at a sitting and still be skinny as a stick. She says that she's "a connoisseur of frozen desserts." At least she used to say that.

"I'll treat you, Kate," Pam said. "It's my celebration."

"Thanks, Pam," Kate said.

I think that since this thing with her parents, Kate doesn't get much of an allowance anymore. I guess she wasn't excited about going because she couldn't afford a Blondie Special. That's a really nice thing about Pam, the way she'll always pay for things. I mean, she gets about ten times the allowance of the rest of us, but she's very generous with it.

I got up to get a drink of water at the water fountain when I heard someone call, "Abigail!" I turned around, and there was Sarah Stern. It was a total shock. I had completely forgotten about her.

"Hi! I was calling and calling you," she said. "I didn't know you had lunch this period. Didn't you find it a fascinating assembly? Greece and Rome are the most romantic places in the world. Especially the way Mr. MacFadden describes them." She pulled a newspaper clipping out of her backpack. "Look," she continued. "I found this article in the paper about the costume exhibit. I thought you might find it interesting." She smiled and handed it to me.

"Gee. Thanks, Sarah," I said.

I looked around. Pamela and the others were watching us from our table. Sarah couldn't see them from behind the pillar, but I could. They probably hadn't heard her mention the museum, but I could tell they were wondering why I was talking to Motormouth. Especially Pamela.

"They have some gorgeous gowns, don't you think?" Sarah said.

I looked quickly at the clipping. There was a picture of a beautiful cape covered in feathers.

"If I had to go to a ball, that's exactly what I

would want to wear," Sarah said, looking over my shoulder. "And they also have ball gowns from the court of France."

"Wow!" I said. I wasn't sure what they wore at the court of France, but I bet it was really something.

"I wonder if they'll have the dress that Marie Antoinette wore on the fateful day of her tragic death," Sarah said, sighing.

"Didn't she have her head cut off?" I asked.

"Well, yes."

"Then I don't think I'd want to see that dress, Sarah." It gave me a shiver up my spine to think about it.

"Well, perhaps not," Sarah admitted. "But I'd love to see something she wore. She was so beautiful, and so full of sorrow."

I looked over at the table again. Pamela made a face at me. I sort of smiled back at her.

"Am I keeping you from an engagement?" Sarah asked.

"Well, it's just some of my friends. We always eat lunch together," I explained.

Sarah peered around the pillar. "Oh, it's Pamela Baldwin and Katherine Tucker." Then she smiled and waved at Pam and Kate. They looked down at their plates. "Hello!" Sarah called to them.

They didn't answer her. I felt sort of embarrassed that they were treating Sarah this way, though Sarah didn't seem to notice.

"What did you think of the Literary Club meeting?" Sarah called out. "Wasn't it thrilling?"

"No," said Pam shortly, to her mashed potatoes.

"I found your story to be quite original," Sarah went on.

"Umph," Pam said.

This conversation was not going well at all. Sarah must have thought so, too.

"Well, I don't want to keep you," she said, turning back to me. She looked very uncomfortable. "Ta." She waved her hand and left.

"Ta," I said.

I went and sat back down at the table and smiled nervously. I knew Pamela would be upset if she thought I was making friends with someone she really hated.

"What was that all about?" Pamela asked, sort of snottily. "I thought you didn't even know old Motormouth."

"I just met her yesterday. She lives on my block," I said.

"So?" Pam said. "That doesn't mean you have to talk to her."

"Pamela!" Beth said, in a mom sort of voice, "Abby would be very rude not to talk to a neighbor. Anyway, I'm sure she's not all that bad. She probably has had some very interesting experiences."

"Beth, you think the school nurse has had some

42

very interesting experiences. Anyway, there's nothing interesting about Motormouth, except how she keeps her tongue flapping all day without biting it off," Pam said.

When Pam doesn't like someone, she *really* doesn't like them.

"Now, what do you think I should wear tonight, my blue minidress or my black skirt with the ruffle?" she continued.

For the rest of lunch we talked about Pamela's meeting with Denver James. We decided she should wear her blue dress, and that she should say, "Very pleased to meet you. I enjoy the show," when she shook his hand. Beth wanted her to say, "I absolutely adore you on the show," but we thought that was a little too much. We also decided she should wear her hair up, because it made her look older, and that she could say the autograph was for "some of my friends." It was mostly me and Beth and Pamela making these decisions. Kate hardly said anything the whole meal, and she hardly ate anything, either.

"All right," said Pamela, when we were finished eating. "I call a meeting of the For Blondes Only club for tomorrow at two o'clock at my house so I can tell you everything that happened."

"Okay," said Kate.

"Could we make it two-thirty?" asked Beth. "I've got to go to these auditions in the morning."

"Beth! What's more important? The seventh-grade musical, or Denver James?" Pamela asked. "Okay, two-thirty, but you're not getting any of Lucia's new pizza dip. What about it, Abs?"

I didn't know what to say. This was going to be the most important FBO meeting in history, and I had made a date with Sarah Stern the Motormouth. To go to a museum.

"Abby? Is there a problem?" Pamela asked.

I didn't know what to do. I thought for a second about canceling out on Sarah. After all, we could go to the museum some other time. She probably wouldn't mind. I could just tell her my mom was sick. That's what I would do: I would tell her my mom was sick and couldn't take us. Of course, then *her* mom would probably offer to take us, and what would I do? Or she would send my mother a get well *poem* or something, and my mom would find out I'd lied. The thing is, I'm a very bad liar. Every time I try to lie, I always screw it up somehow. I knew I would get found out, and Sarah's feelings would be hurt, and I would get in trouble, and it would be a big mess. Why did I ask Sarah to the museum in the first place? I'm such a jerk, I thought.

"Abby!" Pamela said. "What is the matter with you? I asked you a question."

"Sorry, Pam," I said. "I was just thinking."

"Well, stop thinking all the time. It gets on people's nerves. Listen, is two-thirty tomorrow okay, or what?" she replied.

"Actually, I'm kind of busy all day tomorrow," I said, diving right in.

"Doing what?"

"Well, I have to go to a museum. With my mother," I said.

"Why?" Pam asked.

"Well, she wants me to see this costume exhibit. You know. Mothers." That sounded pretty good. I would accept that excuse if I were Pam. Of course, the problem was I'm not Pam.

"Well, tell her you can't go," Pam said. "Your mom won't mind. You can just go another time, can't you?"

The problem was that everyone knows my mother isn't really strict. She would never make me do something like go to a museum if I didn't want to. I'd never thought I would wish for a stricter mother.

"Well, no. See, we kind of invited someone to come with us. I mean, my mom invited her, this person, to come, and so I can't get out of it."

The girls all looked at me, very curious. This wasn't going very well at all. I knew they would not rest until they knew who was coming with me. They're like that. And I knew I would let it slip somehow, I'm such a lousy liar. So I just told the truth. Sort of.

"She invited that Sarah, uh, Motormouth Stern, actually," I said. "I couldn't believe she would do something like that, but I really have to go, or

45

she'd say I was rude or something. I mean, I can't get out of it."

"Abby! That's so awful," Kate said.

"Yes, it's terrible, isn't it? I didn't know what to say when she told me about it. I guess she just felt sorry for Sarah, uh, Motormouth or something. You know what a nice person my mom is," I said.

This was working okay. It wasn't *exactly* a lie, exactly. And now the FBO club was feeling pretty sorry for me. Except Pamela. She was a little bit annoyed.

"Abby," she said, "you're such a pushover. You should never let people walk all over you like that. I mean if my mother ever had the nerve . . . not that she would ever dream of making me do anything like that . . . but that's because I would just say 'No.' You have to learn to stand up for yourself."

"Pam, not everyone is as brave as you are," Beth said. "Don't worry about it, Abby. We understand. Anyway, I'm sure Motormouth's not all that bad. Maybe it will be fun."

"I wouldn't bet on that," said Pam.

"Poor Abby!" Kate sighed.

"Well, I'll manage," I said. "It's only for one day, after all."

"Well, we'll just have to wait until tomorrow night then," Pamela decided. "Though it really stinks, Abs." She got up to go. Then she turned to Kate, and said, "Katie, maybe you could come over early Saturday, and we could spend the day together. I know just the thing to cheer you up. We can give each other manicures and maybe go to the frozen yogurt shop for raspberry ripple. Okay?"

"Okay, Pam," Kate said. "I'd love to."

Pam put her arm around Kate, and they walked out together. I sighed. I knew Pam must be pretty angry with me for making her wait on Saturday. But it could have been worse. At least now I could go to the museum with Sarah without sneaking around. For the rest of the day I actually felt pretty good about everything. I could spend the day with Sarah, and then go see the FBO club in the evening, and no one had to know it was my idea to ask Sarah in the first place.

I was in a good mood when I was heading home. We'd had a great time at Cone Heaven. Beth had a copy of the script for the play, so we were all helping her practice her scene for tomorrow's audition. I thought she really had a chance, she's so good. Pamela was doing all the boys' parts in this really deep funny voice, and then Kate laughed so hard at one point that ice cream came out of her nose. It made me really happy to see that. Kate used to laugh like that all the time, before the divorce.

I was even looking forward to dinner, because on Friday my mom sometimes orders out for pizza, and we don't have to put Texas Paul's sauce on it. Although Paul likes it better that way. Really. I was walking around the corner when I saw Sarah sitting on her porch, reading.

"Hi, Sarah," I said.

"Hi, Abigail. I'm reading the most interesting book. It's about how Lord Ivo joins a band of smugglers and gets caught and sent to prison, and the only person who can rescue him is the brave and beautiful Ravenna Hazelwood, but she's being kidnapped by highwaymen right now, so it doesn't look too good. You should hear the description of the dress she wears to the evil Lady Ashbury's ball. It sounds just like some of the ones we're seeing tomorrow. I'm very thrilled about that."

"Me, too. I'll see you at ten-fifteen, right?" I said.

"Yes, I'm looking forward to meeting your parents. I've seen them going in and out, and they look like such charming people. Is your father on television? I believe I've seen someone who looks just like him selling sauce."

"My stepfather. Yes, he's Texas Paul," I replied.

"How exciting," said Sarah. "My father's a lawyer. It's terribly dull, not like on TV or anything. He never goes to court, just to the office. It's been a great disappointment to me." Sarah sighed.

"Well, eating barbeque sauce all the time isn't

too exciting, really. You get pretty sick of it," I said.

"Surely you don't eat it all the time."

I was starting to get used to the way she talked, but I have to admit it did sound funny coming from this kid in blue jeans. She sounded as if she were always at a ball.

"Yes, we eat it *all the time*. On spaghetti, on chicken, on everything."

"Donuts?" Sarah said.

"Waffles," I replied.

Sarah laughed. "Now you're joking with me."

"No, my mom actually served us waffles and sauce one day. I think she was out of syrup." This was true. Actually, it had tasted okay, but I wouldn't exactly eat it every day.

"Gross me out," Sarah said. It was the most normal thing I had ever heard her say. I guess she was too shocked to think of something fancy.

"We're allowed a day off now and then," I said. "But Paul puts it on everything. He really likes it."

"Well, at least he makes barbeque sauce. What if it were something like frog's legs?"

"Or sheep's eyes," I said.

"Or even chocolate sauce — try eating *that* on spaghetti. You'd become terribly fat," Sarah replied. "All of this food talk leaves me starved. May I offer you some Oreos?"

"Actually, I have to get going," I said. "But I'll see you tomorrow."

"Perfect," said Sarah. "As long as you promise I don't have to eat any waffles."

She waved good-bye, and went into her house. I was starting to feel kind of funny. I walked over to my house with this big lump in my stomach, and I couldn't even enjoy the pizza at dinner very much. The thing is, I felt pretty bad about saying all those things at lunch — that my mom had invited Sarah, and calling her Motormouth and everything. It didn't seem so terrible at the time, but it really was. I liked Sarah. It was pretty mean to talk about her behind her back like that. It made me wish I had just stuck up for my own ideas like Mom had said. That's the thing about lying. If you don't get in trouble for it, you feel bad about it anyway.

4

That night I had this great dream that I got to meet Denver James. He was a really big fan of Texas Paul's Bar-B-Que, and he did a commercial for Paul and said *"Yippee-ii-aay"* and everything. Then, when he met me, he said, "Why, you're even prettier than your friend Pamela." That's when I knew it was a dream. Nobody would ever think I was prettier than Pamela, except maybe my mother, who always says I don't have enough self-confidence. Anyway, as soon as I realized I was dreaming, I woke right up and remembered it was the day Sarah Stern and I were going to the museum to see the costume exhibit.

I looked at the clock. It was nine o'clock, and I had told Sarah to be at my house by ten-fifteen so we could make our train. That didn't give me very much time to get ready. I always have a hard time deciding what clothes to wear. Even if I'm just going to Pamela's house, or to the super-market with my mother, it takes me forever to pick out the right outfit. Once I took half an hour deciding between red and green socks to wear with my gym shorts at school. The way I see it, you never know who you might run into, and going into New York City, I knew I had to look absolutely perfect. What if I accidently ran into Denver James? He lives in New York. Maybe he's really into nineteenth-century clothes. And maybe he would overhear me talking to Sarah about Texas Paul's and he would say, "Why, that's my favorite sauce, and you're even prettier than Pamela." I thought about that for a while. Quite a long while. Then, by the time I finally made up my mind about what to wear, changed it four times, and got dressed, it was ten o'clock and my mother was calling me for breakfast. So I never had a chance to call Pamela and find out what happened when she met Denver James.

We were all sitting at the breakfast table eating eggs 'n' sauce when Sarah knocked on the door. I thought she was going to burst out laughing when Mom asked her if she'd like to try some. I pinched her really hard under the table, though, so she didn't get a chance to laugh. Actually, I think Paul and my mom liked Sarah. She was very polite, and she didn't say anything too weird, except that she enjoyed Paul's commercials, "particularly the very amusing outfit you wear." I was very impressed when she said that. Sometimes being polite means you have to lie a little bit, and

I could see that Sarah was good at politeness. Paul certainly thought so. His face practically split apart, he was smiling so hard. I don't think anyone ever told him they liked his commercials before.

My mom took about a million hours to get her coat and keys, and tell Paul what to have for lunch and how to work the washing machine and things like that. She thinks no one in the whole family can do anything without her around. Halfway to the train station she wanted to turn around to remind him that Michael only ate American cheese for lunch, but I convinced her not to. Finally we made it to the station and onto the train, which pulled up just as we got there.

"Just in the nick of time," Sarah said. "Lord Ivo is always doing things just in the nick of time. Especially saving people from certain death. He's very lucky that way."

"Oh, Lord Ivo!" my mother said. "I loved those Lord Ivo books when I was young. They were so exciting and romantic. And he was so dashing!"

"He still is," Sarah replied.

I couldn't believe it. For the whole rest of the train ride, Sarah and my mom talked about Lord Ivo this and Lord Ivo that. I was really amazed. I mean, sometimes my mom can be annoying, but mostly I really like her. She's funny and smart and pretty, and I think she's the best mom of any of the moms I know. It made me think maybe Sarah wasn't so weird with all this Lord Ivo stuff after all. It made me really curious to read that book she'd given me, *Antonia of the Night*. In fact, I thought Pamela might like these books, even though I knew she would never be caught dead doing anything Sarah liked to do. They sounded sort of like *Your Life to Lead*, only everyone wears fancy dresses and there are pirates.

Anyway, by the time we got to the museum, I knew more about Lord Ivo than I ever thought I would know. Fortunately, my mom had some shopping to do, or I might have had to spend the whole day listening to them talk about his life. He sounded really interesting and everything, but I was feeling a little bit left out.

I love going to the Metropolitan Museum. I love the way it sounds inside. There are tons of people everywhere, but it's so big, it sort of echoes. I love the beautiful flowers in the big entrance hall, and I love the buttons you wear to prove that you've paid. I was going to clip mine to my shirt as I always do, but Sarah clipped hers onto her hairband, just to make me laugh. So I clipped mine to my ear, like an earring, to make her laugh, and that's how we wore them the whole day.

We were having so much fun goofing around with the buttons that we didn't pay too much attention to the museum lady who gave us directions to the costumes. It's a very big museum, and we got lost in about a second.

"Did she say upstairs or down?" I asked Sarah.

"Downstairs, I think. But I don't recall her mentioning mummies," Sarah replied. We were standing in the mummy room.

"No, I thought she said something about Greece," I said.

"Rome," said Sarah.

"May I help you ladies with something?" a voice asked.

I turned around, and standing behind me was the cutest guy I had ever seen. He was about eighteen, and he had beautiful green eyes, curly black hair, and a perfect smile. At first I was stunned. Why would this adorable guy be talking to me? But then I noticed his uniform and realized he was a guard at the museum.

I was too shy to say anything to anyone that cute, so I looked at Sarah. She was just as in love as I was. Her mouth was sort of open, and she had a real funny look on her face. I kicked her. It seemed to help. "We're looking for the, umm, ballrooms, I mean ball gowns," she said.

"Yes," I said.

"Okay, ladies," he said, smiling again. He was so cute I couldn't believe it. He was cuter than Denver James almost. "Just blah blah blah blah blah."

That's not what he said exactly, but that's what it sounded like to me. I was so busy staring at his beautiful eyes, I couldn't pay any attention to the directions.

"Thank you," said Sarah.

"Thank you," I said.

He walked away. Even in the dopey uniform the guards wear, he looked great.

"Wow," I said.

"Wow," said Sarah.

We watched until he turned the corner. Then we stared at the corner for a while. Then we looked at each other.

"Did you hear what he told us?" Sarah asked.

"No," I said.

"Neither did I," Sarah said. "I was too over-whelmed. He looks like Lord Ivo. Only younger. And with hazel eyes."

"Green," I said.

"Grayish-green," Sarah said.

"What should we do now?" I asked.

"Well, we'll just have to ask someone else. Someone old."

"A woman," I said.

"An old woman," Sarah said.

Unfortunately, there weren't any old women around. We walked through the mummy room to the hieroglyphics room, but we still didn't see any-one to ask. Then we came to the temple room, where there's this big Egyptian temple from a million years ago. And there he was again. Sitting on the steps of the temple. Eating a sandwich.

Sarah and I both stopped short. Then, without even saying a word, we started to back out of the room. Both of us were too embarrassed to ask for directions again. We had almost made it to the door when I tripped and fell down with this terrific thud.

"Abigail, are you all right?" Sarah asked.

"Are you okay?" Mr. Gorgeous Guard said, running over to me. He reached out his hand to help me up.

"I'm fine," I said. "Really."

I waved his hand away and got up by myself. Actually I had fallen pretty hard on my behind, but I wasn't going to mention that. I didn't want him to think I had hurt myself. For some reason, that would have been even more humiliating. Though I felt humiliated enough, believe me.

"Couldn't you girls find the costume exhibit?" he asked.

I didn't know what to say. "Well, we were too busy falling in love with your smile to hear what you said" sounded pretty stupid. Fortunately, Sarah took over. "It's my fault," she said. "I have absolutely no sense of direction."

"Yeah," said Mr. Gorgeous. "I know how you feel. When I first started working here, I couldn't find anything. Listen, I'm on my break right now. Why don't I walk you girls over?"

"Thank you," said Sarah. "That's most chivalrous of you."

Mr. Gorgeous smiled when she said that. I guess he didn't expect a kid to use such a big word. It made me feel kind of proud to be with her.

"Have you worked here long?" Sarah asked him.

"No, just a few months," he said. "I go to Fordham University, but I need this job to pay for books and stuff. It's a nice place to work. I like to look at the paintings."

"I like the knights on horseback," Sarah said. "They're so romantic."

"And what do you like?" he asked, looking at me.

I didn't know what to say. Once again, Sarah saved me. "Abigail is a very talented dress designer. That's why we're going to look at the costumes."

"Yeah? That's nice, Abigail." When he said it, it sounded like the most beautiful name in the world. "Well, here we are, girls, right down those stairs are the costumes."

"Thank you," said Sarah.

"It was my pleasure. Good-bye, Abigail. Good-bye. . . ."

"Sarah," said Sarah.

"Good-bye, Sarah. I'm Al. I hope you enjoy your visit."

"Good-bye, Al," Sarah said.

"Good-bye," I said. Finally I was able to talk just when he was leaving.

After he had turned the corner, Sarah and I looked at each other. Then we both screamed, sort of a quiet, museum kind of scream. Then we laughed.

"Al," I said.

"Alexander," Sarah said as we walked down the stairs. "What a perfect name."

The costume exhibit was set up like a giant ballroom. There were chandeliers, and music was playing in the background, and all the mannequins, wearing their beautiful clothes, were set up as if they were dancing with each other. It was like a fantasy world.

"Oh, Abigail!" Sarah gasped. "This must be what it feels like to make your debut at a ball. In a white lace dress."

"With a heart-shaped neckline, and beads all over it." There was a dress like that in the center of the room.

"You make your bow to the queen," Sarah continued. "Then, shaking with nerves, you look at the dance floor. A man comes over to you. He has black hair and hazel eyes."

"Green!" I said.

"Oh, all right. Green. He asks you for this dance and, curtseying, you graciously accept his most kind invitation. His name is . . ."

"ALEXANDER!" We both said at the same time. Then we laughed.

"He's an Italian prince," Sarah said.

"But he's in disguise," I added.

"Because of the evil duke, who wants to murder him."

"Why?" I asked.

"I don't know. We'll have to discover his evil plan later," Sarah said. "This is fun, I've never had anyone help me write a story before."

"I've never written a story before."

"Well, I think you have flair, Abigail."

"I don't know. I'm better at drawing than I am at writing," I said. But I liked it that she told me I had flair.

"Well, you can draw all the characters," Sarah said. "We'll start with the evil duke. Or should he be a marquis?"

"What's a marquis?" I asked.

"It's one under a duke," Sarah said.

"How do you know that?"

"Well, they're all over the Lord Ivo books. Anyway, I like English history. I want to go to England more than anything, and see where the Queen lives."

"Pamela went to England with her father and mother last year. She said it was boring, and the food was lousy."

"Well, *I* wouldn't think it was boring," Sarah said, as if Pamela's opinion had to be wrong.

It's funny — I was so worried about what Pamela would think about Sarah, I never thought that Sarah might not like Pamela, either. It made me feel kind of bad. I never had any friends before who didn't like each other. I could see that it might be kind of uncomfortable.

"Well, I think marquis sounds more evil," I said.

"Okay," said Sarah. "The evil uncle can be the Marquis of Brisbane. That sounds wicked. I wish we had a notebook so we could write this down."

For the rest of the afternoon we planned our story. Our heroine's name was Annabella. Sarah said all the heroines have long fancy names like that. She was beautiful and fair, but had a fiery temper. That was my idea. I didn't think I could write a story about a wimp. Alexander, the disguised Italian prince, was tall and dark and devastatingly handsome. He had a poetic soul and a way with women.

While we walked through the exhibit, we decided on all the clothes that Annabella should wear. Then afterwards, when my mom picked us up, we had lunch at the museum café. Sarah ordered watercress sandwiches, just to try them, but she didn't like them very much, so we shared my tuna salad.

We kept right on talking about the story, though. We couldn't decide how our hero and heroine should meet. Sarah thought he should rescue her from highwaymen. But I thought they should meet at a ball. That way, I could design a great dress for her. I couldn't wait to get back home so that I could get my sketchbook and draw it.

"Do you want to come to dinner at my house tonight?" Sarah said, sort of shyly. "We could work on the story some more."

"Sure, I'd love to!" I said. "If it's okay with you, Mom?"

"Of course," Mom said. "I wasn't planning anything special."

She got up to pay the check, and Sarah leaned over and whispered, "Don't worry, there's no barbeque sauce on anything my mom cooks."

Actually, Sarah's mom turned out to be this absolutely great cook, and also a very nice lady. Sarah's mom is a lawyer, too, just like Sarah's dad, so on Saturdays they always have this big family dinner, and her parents take turns cooking. Sarah says it's the only time all week that everyone is home at the same time. Both of her parents work long hours, so when she comes home from school she has to hang out with her two older brothers. They're both in high school. She has a brother named Sam, and one named Simon. Her parents are named Saul and Sandra. Sam, Simon, Saul, Sandra, and Sarah Stern. Sarah thinks it's "utterly ridiculous," but I think it's sort of funny and nice.

I wasn't sure what to expect, but Sarah's family was pretty normal, and I thought her brothers were kind of cute. Sam is seventeen and Simon is fourteen and she thinks they're "dreadfully obnoxious," mostly because they both call her Worm. They both seemed more interested in sports than in books, and they spent most of dinner talking about a basketball game with her father, while her mom asked me those typical mom kind of questions, like what my favorite subject is in school, and how I like the neighborhood. Then, after dinner, Sarah had a big fight with Simon about whose turn it was to clean up. She was so mad, she dropped all of her fancy words and sounded just like I do when I fight with Michael. In the end, her mom told Simon to do the dishes because Sarah had a guest, and we escaped up to her room with huge bowls of chocolate ice cream.

"I loathe brothers," Sarah said.

"They're not so bad, Sarah. At least you have *older* brothers."

"What's so great about that?" she asked. "They just boss you around."

"Yeah, but they can introduce you to their cute friends. My brother's friends spend all their time watching cartoons and playing video games."

"Well, Simon does have a friend named David who's quite appealing," Sarah said. "But he never pays any attention to me."

She leaned back on her bed and sighed. Sarah has exactly the kind of bedroom I pictured her having. It's so beautiful and romantic. She has wallpaper with lavender flowers all over it, and a lavender rug. She has a huge canopy bed with big fluffy lace pillows, and a white lace canopy. She even has a big window with a padded window seat. She has a desk in the corner piled high with papers, and she has books everywhere: on her shelves, on her nightstand, under her bed, on the floor. I never saw so many books in my life. She also has a store of junk food in her closet that is truly amazing. It's the perfect room to hang around in and talk about love.

"Well, maybe one day David will notice you, Sarah," I said.

"Yes. One day, he'll suddenly look at me and say, 'Why Sarah, I never realized how truly beauteous you are.' "

"He'll lean over to kiss you," I said, giggling.

"Too late!" Sarah said. "For I will be engaged to marry my beloved."

"Al, the museum guard," I said, laughing harder.

"*Alexander.*"

"Albert," I said. "Alan, Alfred."

Sarah threw her pillow at me and fell over, laughing. She had the funniest laugh I'd ever heard. It sounded like, "Whoop, whoop, whoop." Just hearing it made me laugh even harder.

"Oh, Abigail," she said between whoops. "His name couldn't be Alfred."

"Aloysius," I suggested.

Aloysius was the name of Denver James's great-uncle from Britain who died, leaving all his money to Denver. But his evil twin, Dallas James, hid the will and . . .

"Oh, no!" I suddenly said.

I had forgotten all about Denver James. I couldn't believe it. Pamela was going to be furious at me. I looked at my watch. It was eight o'clock.

"Sarah, I'm really sorry. I have to go home right away. I forgot something very important," I said.

Sarah was a little surprised, but I didn't have time to explain. I just grabbed my coat and ran out the door and down the street to my house. When I got there, Paul was sitting at the kitchen table, just hanging up the phone.

"Abster, that was for you," he said.

"Was it Pamela?" I asked breathlessly.

"Yes, it was."

"What did you tell her?" I asked, holding my breath.

If Pamela knew I had stood her up for Motor-mouth Stern, she would never forgive me.

"I just told her you weren't home."

"Did you tell her where I was?" I asked.

"No," Paul said. "Why?"

I put my arms around him and kissed him about a million times. He left the kitchen with a goofy smile on his face. I love Paul. I would have to think up something to tell Pamela, but at least she didn't know I had ditched her. Maybe I could save the day after all. I picked up the phone and dialed Pam's number.

"Hello?" Pam said.

"Pam? It's me, Abby."

"Abby, where are you? I'm totally furious at you."

"My mom made us stop at Granny Gargul's for dinner," I said, thinking up a lie as fast as I could. It's amazing how much better you get with practice. "I couldn't get out of it."

Granny Gargul is Paul's mother. When my mom first married Paul, I was really embarrassed that her name was Gargul like his, but now I'm used to it. Anyway, Granny Gargul lives in New York, so it would make sense that we had to eat there. She's this very nice old lady who always gives me slips and panties for Christmas. Sometimes I understand why Paul is a little odd.

"The underwear lady?" Pam said. "Oh, Abby, I don't believe it."

"You don't?" Maybe it wasn't such a great lie after all.

"No! I had so much to tell you," Pam said.

"Well, why don't I come over now?" I felt just terrible, hearing how disappointed Pam sounded.

"There's no point. Beth and Kate have to leave in a few minutes anyway."

"Well, what about tomorrow, then?" I suggested.

"I'm going shopping with my mother tomorrow."

"Well, I guess I'll see you in school on Monday, then."

"I guess so," Pam said. "Bye."

She hung up the phone. I just sat at the kitchen table feeling depressed. Everything was such a mess. I hated lying all the time. And I hated it that I couldn't tell Pam about Al the museum guard or Sarah's bedroom, or our book. I just wished we all could be friends.

"I'll have to tell Granny Gargul how much we enjoyed dinner," my mom said.

I turned around. She was standing in the kitchen doorway with sort of a sad look on her face.

"I guess you heard me, huh," I said. "Mom, I hate lying, but if Pam knew I forgot to come over because of Sarah Stern . . . she hates Sarah. She calls her Motormouth."

"Well, I think she might be more hurt if she knew you were lying to her."

"So what should I do?" I asked.

"I don't know, honey. But I think you should start being honest about how you feel and what you think. I'm sure Pam would like Sarah if she gave her a chance." She leaned over and kissed me. "Try not to worry so much about everything, sweetie. It will all work itself out," she said as she left.

"It will all work itself out." My mom always says that, but it doesn't really make you feel too much better. I couldn't see any way this was going to work out anytime soon.

5

I spent so much time feeling bad about Pam that I almost completely forgot I had a dentist appointment on Monday morning, and would miss the first half of school. Usually my mom has to drag me kicking and screaming into the dentist's office, but I was so relieved I wouldn't have to see the club in homeroom that I was dressed and waiting in the car before she'd even finished her coffee.

My dentist's name is Dr. White, though I don't believe that's his real name. I think he changed it when he decided to become a dentist. That way, he can drive his patients crazy by saying, "Let Dr. White keep 'em white," while he scrapes away at their teeth. During most visits I want to take his little scraper and stick it in his eye, but that day I was practically praying I had thirty cavities and wouldn't be able to go to school at all. Unfortunately, I didn't even have one, so Mom dropped me off at school in the middle of lunch period, and I went down to find my class in the cafeteria.

The cafeteria smelled the way it always did, a combination of garbage and dirty sneakers. I could see Pamela, Beth, and Kate sitting at our usual table by the water fountain, leaning over their lunches and talking with their heads all close together. On any other day I would have just walked on over and plopped myself down next to one of them, but that day I just didn't feel like it. I felt too guilty.

I'm the worst friend in the entire world, I thought as I watched Beth laugh at something Pam said. I wondered if there was any way that I could sneak out without them seeing me. The back door to the stairs was right past the dessert rack. If I tucked my head into my shoulders, and crept very quietly, I could probably make it without being caught. I pulled the collar of my shirt up over my chin and took a step.

"Hey, Abby!"

Oh, no. Beth had spotted me by the Jell-O squares, and now Pamela and Kate were waving at me, too. Well, there wasn't any choice. I headed over to the table.

This must be how poor Marie Antoinette felt on her way to the guillotine, I thought. My stomach was all in flutters. I felt the way I did when I knew Mom was really mad at me, or when I hadn't studied for a major test. I stared at my

Reeboks and wondered how I would convince the FBO club that I hadn't meant to lie to them and do stuff behind their backs.

"Abby Wagner! Where have you been all morning?" demanded Pamela, chomping on a French fry. "We have the most incredible news in the entire universe!"

I looked at her, surprised. This was not exactly the greeting I was expecting.

"Get this. My mother said I could have my twelfth birthday party on the set!" Pam squealed.

"And Denver James is going to be there," Kate squealed.

"And *I* got called back for the seventh-grade musical," Beth squealed.

"Isn't it just too much?" Kate squealed.

And then they all squealed together.

"I'm so glad you're here," Pamela said, pulling me down in the chair next to her. "I mean, I didn't think I could wait another second before I told you. Isn't this unbelievable?" She squeezed my hand.

"It's probably the greatest day in the life of the FBO club," said Beth.

"We were really worried that you wouldn't come," Kate said, pushing the plate of fries over for me to share. "Are you feeling okay?"

Was I feeling okay? I was feeling like I could hug every one of them for not calling me a liar and hating my guts. I was feeling like dancing on the table and shouting "Long live the For Blondes Only club!" at the top of my lungs. I was feeling that these were the best possible friends I could ever have in the whole world.

I was about to open my mouth and tell them that it was indeed the greatest day in FBO history when I heard a familiar voice.

"Abigail!"

Oh, no. It was Sarah waving at me from the cafeteria line. I'd forgotten that she had fifth-period lunch.

"Gosh, Abby, is she still hanging around?" asked Pam snottily.

"I hope she doesn't think she can sit with us," said Kate.

"She probably thinks she's your friend now that your mom made you go to the museum together," Pam continued.

"Oh, don't be so mean," said Beth.

"Yeah, come on, you guys," I said, standing up so quickly that I banged my thighs on the table. "She's just, uh, saying hello, you know." I crashed into a chair.

"Where are you going, Abby?" asked Pamela. "Sit down. Let's talk about the party."

"And the play," said Beth. "You're not going to believe the cute guys who tried out, and Mr. Harper was telling the most interesting story about his father, who used to be a mime and —"

"I'll be right back. Really," I interrupted, and

hurried toward Sarah, nearly slipping on a tray that was left on the floor. "I'm just going to get some, uh, Jell-O," I said over my shoulder. "Anybody want any?"

I didn't even wait for an answer. I wanted to get to Sarah before she got to the FBO club. If she said anything about our weekend, I was dead.

Sarah was deciding between the chocolate pudding and the pound cake when I reached her. Her tray was already piled high with food, including two sandwiches, some corn and peas, and a bag of chips. Even though I wished she didn't have the same lunch period as the club, seeing her planning to eat all that stuff made me smile.

"Oh, Abigail, I'm so delighted to see you. I have been trying to find you all morning. Were you ill?"

"I had to go to the dentist," I said, with one eye on Pamela, Beth, and Kate. I knew they were watching me.

"My condolences," Sarah said.

"Oh, it was okay. No cavities." I wanted to make this a short conversation.

"Do you feel like hearing my new ideas for Annabella and Alexander?" she asked, heading over toward a table near the front. I guess she knew better than to try to sit at the FBO table. Or maybe she just didn't want to. "I've entirely forsaken the highwaymen. I think they should meet at a beheading."

"A beheading!" I said. "That's not very romantic."

I glanced over at the girls, but they were hunched over talking again. Good, I thought. I've got another minute or two.

"Well, what if it's Alexander who is about to be beheaded?" Sarah continued. "And Annabella's eyes meet his just moments before the ax is dropped."

"Yeah," I said, getting excited. "And then she saves him by bribing the head-chopper guy with jewels."

"The executioner," Sarah corrected.

"Right, the executioner."

I liked this beheading idea. It was nice and gory, and I could just imagine Annabella in a beautiful gold gown, standing in the crowd, gasping as Alexander was about to bite it.

"But why is Alexander going to be beheaded?" I asked.

"How about if Annabella's uncle, the Marquis, wants to keep them apart?" Sarah suggested.

"But they're not even together yet."

"A soothsayer could have forseen their love and warned the uncle of its dire consequences for him," said Sarah.

"Oh, Sarah, that's perfect! I love that."

By now, I was sitting beside Sarah at her table, nibbling one half of her cheese sandwich. I didn't even realize how long I had been there until I heard someone clear their throat just behind me. I turned around to find Kate, standing there with her hands on her hips.

"Hello, Abby," said Kate. "Hello, Sarah."

"Hello," Sarah said.

"Pamela is trying to decide who to invite to her party," said Kate, looking directly at me. "She thought you might want to discuss it."

"Oh, uh, I, uh, was just coming," I said.

"I didn't mean to keep you from your friends," Sarah said.

"Oh, you didn't," I said. "I mean, I wanted to talk to you about . . . I just have to finish up with . . . Pamela's having this party, and . . ."

I felt like a jerk stumbling around like that, looking for the right thing to say. The problem was, there was no right thing. I felt terrible about walking away from Sarah right in the middle of our conversation. But Kate was waiting with her arms folded. I knew Pamela was watching to see what I would do.

"Let's go, Abby," Kate said.

I couldn't tell if Kate was really mad about me talking to Sarah, or if she was just doing this because Pamela had told her to. Not that it mattered. She was still being obnoxious.

"Sarah, I'll, uh. . . ."

"It's all right, Abigail. We'll talk later," Sarah

said. She smiled at me, but I could tell she didn't really feel like smiling. I followed Kate back to the FBO table, hating myself.

Pamela was glaring at me.

"Sorry I had to pull you away from old Motor-mouth," she said sarcastically. "Was she reading you one of her poems?"

I didn't say anything.

"Well, I'm sure whatever you two were talking about was much more interesting than my birthday party in a real-live television studio. Or Beth's big opportunity to star in the seventh-grade musical," she continued.

I knew she didn't really think that Beth's callback was anywhere near as important as her birthday party. She had just thrown that in to make sure Beth would be angry with me, too.

"She just had a question about something we'd seen at the museum," I said.

Pam made a face when I said "museum" like she had smelled something gross. "I guess you two are real buddy-buddy now."

"She's not so bad, Pam," I said.

"Oh, please, Abby. Spare me," said Pam with a little sneer. "You barely know the girl. I spent an entire summer listening to her and her stupid writing."

"Gee, Pam," I said, rather meanly, I must admit. "I seem to remember something about her stupid writing winning color war."

Pam gave me an incredibly dirty look.

"Hey, look, you guys," Beth said, to change the subject. "There's Marco Hernandez. I think he might get the lead in the play. Isn't he gorgeous?"

We all turned in the direction of a tall dark boy wearing a denim jacket and cowboy boots. I thought Pamela was trying to catch my eye, but I wouldn't look at her.

"Hot stuff, Beth," Kate said.

"If I get the lead, I might actually get to kiss him," Beth said dreamily. "Right on stage."

"Gosh, Beth, then your mother would see you," said Kate.

"So what, Kate?" Pamela said.

I could tell she was not in the mood for this conversation. When Pam is angry, she takes it out on the whole world.

"Anyway, if you did get to kiss him, it wouldn't be a real kiss," Pam went on. "I mean, please. Do you think Marco Hernandez would ever kiss a sixth grader?"

Beth looked at her plate.

"No offense, Beth." Pam smiled.

"Yeah, right, Pam," Beth said, with an edge in her voice. "I know."

"So, anyway," Pamela said, looking around the table at each of us, except me. "My party."

"I can't wait," said Kate. "I wish it were sooner."

"I know," said Pamela. "Two weeks is forever.

Still, there's a lot of planning to do."

"Like what?" I said. I probably should have been trying to make up, but I just didn't feel like it. I couldn't help it. Sometimes I get so sick of the world revolving around Pamela.

"Like if we want to invite any boys," said Beth.

Beth was such a good sport. If Pam had just been mean to me like she'd been to Beth, I wouldn't have wanted to talk about her dumb old party.

"Do you think we should?" asked Kate. "What about Denver James?"

"Well, he'll probably be spending most of the time with me, wouldn't you think?" said Pamela. "I mean, it's *my* birthday. I think we'd better invite some other boys for you girls to talk to."

"Oh," said Kate.

I could tell she was disappointed. Though I don't know what she'd expected. Frankly, even though Pamela is incredibly beautiful, and the writer's daughter, I would be surprised if Denver James would even want to hang out with her. I mean, she is only twelve.

Beth didn't seem to care much about Denver James. "Well, I think we ought to invite Benny Morito and Josh Baron and" — she glanced up at the clock on the cafeteria wall — "Oh, my gosh, look. It's time for the audition. Wish me luck. And don't kill each other while I'm gone, okay?" she said with a smile. Smoothing her sweater over her jeans, Beth grabbed her bookbag and headed toward the door.

"Good luck, Beth," Kate and I called after her.

"Break a leg," said Pam.

We watched Beth round the corner on her way to the auditorium. I took a deep breath. I was nervous for her. I really, truly hoped that she would get a part.

"Now then," Pamela said, turning to Kate as if I were invisible. "Back to important matters."

Maybe it was because Pamela was ignoring me anyway, or maybe it was because I just wasn't that interested in her party, but whatever the reason, I was having a hard time even listening to the conversation. I kept thinking about Annabella and Alexander, and how difficult it would be to have an evil uncle who wanted to cut your boyfriend's head off, and how beautiful Annabella would look in her golden gown, as long as it didn't get splattered with blood. Without even knowing it, I must have picked up a pencil and started sketching Annabella in her beheading outfit.

I was drawing little beads on the sleeve when I noticed that Pamela was talking to me.

"Excuse us for boring you, Ms. Wagner," she said.

"Huh?"

"It's pretty obvious that you have far more important things to think about than my birthday party," she said. "Like your little doodles."

"They're not doodles, Pam. They're sketches."

"Yes, well, I know you think so," said Pam nastily. "And, certainly, Kate and I wouldn't want to keep you from your very serious work, would we, Katie? I have an idea. Why don't you just let us know when you find the time to talk with us." Pamela stood up and flipped her hair over her shoulders. I didn't know if she was waiting for me to say something, but I couldn't think of anything to say.

"Come on, Kate," she said. "Let's leave Ms. Picasso to her art." And with that, she hooked her arm through Kate's and walked straight out the door. Kate glanced back at me over her shoulder, but then Pam must have said something funny, because she turned away and started to laugh. I looked around to see if anyone had witnessed what had just happened. No one seemed to notice me all by myself. Even Sarah must have left the lunchroom. I put down my pencil, stuffed my napkin with Annabella's half-finished gown in my pocket, and bit my nails.

Well, I thought to myself, now what?

6

Even though I wished I could hide in the cafeteria for the rest of the day, I had to go to English class after lunch. Usually I like English a lot, mostly because Mr. MacFadden always looks so adorable, and sometimes he reads poetry to us at the end of class and it sounds really wonderful. Mr. MacFadden is very dramatic. I think sometimes he wishes he were an actor instead of a teacher. Anyway, that day I knew English would be a disaster. I was right. Pamela and Kate wouldn't talk to me or anything. I sit next to Ellen Wu, this girl with really long, beautiful hair that she's always swinging around her head to show off. She kept hitting me in the face with it. Also, she has this really stupid giggle, and she giggles at everything Mr. MacFadden says. It's so annoying.

I was hoping to tell Beth about what happened in the cafeteria, because I knew she would listen to my side of the story. But she had gotten out of class for the auditions, so I couldn't. Pamela kept whispering to Kate all through class, which I knew she was doing just to get back at me. The problem was, it worked. I felt so lonely and left out. I hated it.

By the time the bell rang, I felt just rotten. All I wanted to do was get out of there as fast as I could. So I got up out of my seat and tripped right over Ellen Wu's bookbag and fell flat on my face on the floor, banging my knee really hard at the same time. Some days you should not get out of bed, that's all there is to it.

Mr. MacFadden helped me up. "Abby, I guess that last poem really floored you," he said.

"Oh, Mr. MacFadden, hee hee hee hee hee," Ellen Wu said.

"Are you okay?" Mr. MacFadden asked me.

"Fine," I said, brushing myself off. I looked over at Pamela and Kate. Pam had this sort of nasty smile on her face, as if she thought I had gotten what I deserved.

"All right, everybody, Abby hasn't hurt anything but her dignity, so let's go," Mr. MacFadden said.

Everyone started to file out of the room, talking and laughing. About me, probably. I just hung around until the room emptied out a little. Then I started sort of limping out the door. My knee was killing me.

"Is everything okay, Abby?" Mr. MacFadden

asked. "I noticed you weren't sitting with your usual coterie." Mr. MacFadden always uses words like coterie. I had no idea what it meant, but I figured he was talking about Pamela.

"Yes. Fine, everything's fine," I said. I think Mr. MacFadden is great and everything, but to tell you the truth, I wasn't really up to talking to him about it.

"Okay. You might want to put some ice on your knee when you get home," he said.

"Thanks," I said. I meant it. Some teachers, if they knew you hurt yourself in some embarrassing way, would make this big deal about it, and get you even more embarrassed. I think Mr. MacFadden knew that sometimes hurting your dignity was worse than anything else.

I was limping down the stairs at the front of the school when I heard Sarah calling my name.

"Abigail, Abigail!" She was sitting on the bottom step waving up at me. I limped over to her.

"Abigail, are you all right? You're wounded!"

"I just tripped and fell down in English class. I think I broke my knee."

"Well, you must be in excruciating agony!" she said. "Do you think we ought to call your mother? Perhaps you shouldn't walk."

"No, I'm all right. I just need to rest it for a minute." I sat down next to her on the step.

It was nice to see Sarah. I was so happy to talk to someone who liked me. "I'm having a bad day,"

I said. The understatement of the century.

"You mean one of *those* days?" Sarah asked. "I have those sometimes, where you get out of bed and your favorite shirt is torn, and your mother makes poached eggs for breakfast — "

"With sauce," I added.

"And your brother eats the last bagel — "

"And you lose your math homework — "

"And your cat throws up on your bedspread — " Sarah went on.

"And you're late for school — "

"And you have Mr. Adler first period — "

"Miss Moritz," I said.

"Even worse," Sarah agreed. "And there's a pop quiz."

"Mystery Meat for lunch."

"You forget your gym shorts."

"Two demerits!" We both said together. "Two demerits!" is what Mrs. Hanley in gym always gives you for forgetting your gym shorts.

"You get sent to the principal," I said.

"No, you get arrested!" Sarah was getting a little carried away. "You're falsely accused of murder and sent to the electric chair where you die a horrible death. Is that the kind of day you had?" she asked.

"Worse," I said. We looked at each other. Then she started to whoop. Then we both started to laugh. It was the first time since lunch that I didn't feel totally miserable.

"Oh, gosh, poor Abigail," Sarah said, once she had whooped herself out. "I guess falling down in English was kind of the *coup de grâce*."

"The what?"

"*Coup de grâce*. It's French for 'the final blow.' You know, the one that finishes you off."

"Well, I hope it was. I don't think I could take any more today."

"Well, I've got some good news for you if you're interested," Sarah said. "I've been working on our story all afternoon, and I think I've got a really good beginning written down. Do you want to see?" She pulled her notebook out of her backpack and opened it up. There were about three pages all scribbled in this very messy handwriting. I picked it up and started reading.

Alexander, the Prince of Italy, marched solemnly to certain doom. He held his head high, his black curls glistening in the sun. "Though they may behead me and throw my bloody corpse to the dogs, they cannot break my spirit," he thought to himself. Suddenly, he saw a face in the crowd. . . .

"Well, well, well," I heard a voice behind me say. I looked up. There were Pamela and Kate, looking about as snotty as I had ever seen them look.

"Isn't this sweet," Pam continued. "Ms. Picasso

has a new little friend. I guess that's why she doesn't need her old friends anymore."

"Pam, you're being ridiculous," I said. I couldn't believe this was happening.

"Ridiculous? You're the one who looks ridiculous, hanging around with old Motormouth."

I heard Sarah breathe in really suddenly, like someone had punched her.

"Shut up, Pamela," I said. I looked at Kate, hoping she would say something to make Pam stop, but she just shrugged her shoulders. "Come on, Sarah. Let's go." I looked over at her. She was looking very pale, and she had her teeth sort of clenched together.

"Oh, don't go. Please, we would just love to hear what's so interesting over here. What you just *have* to talk about all day long. Are you writing poems?" Pam asked, and before I could stop her, she snatched the notebook right out of my hand and started looking at it.

"Give it back," I said.

" '*Oh, Alexander . . . Alexander . . . I do love you so,*' " Pamela started to read out loud in this goofy voice. " '*Please, don't let them kill you.*' " She gave the notebook to Kate.

" '*Don't worry, fair lady, they can never kill me, for you hold my heart in your hand,*' " Kate read.

"Eeeeewww, how gross. It must be dripping all over her shirt," Pam said.

86

That made Kate laugh.

Sarah and I just sat there for a minute. I think we were in shock. When we were writing the story together, we both thought it was really great. But now, listening to Pamela make fun of it, it sounded sort of stupid and embarrassing. Sarah was getting paler and paler. It was worse for her because she was the one who had written most of that stuff. Looking at her made me really angry at Pamela. I had never seen her be as mean to anyone as she was being to Sarah.

"Give it back, Pamela," I said.

"Do you want it?" asked Pam. "Here, catch!"

She threw the book right over my head to Kate, who threw it back to her, laughing. I couldn't believe Kate was going along with all this. I knew she was in Pam's shadow, but not this much. They kept that up, throwing it back and forth a couple of times, until suddenly Sarah yelled, "Look out!"

Kate looked, just for a moment, and Sarah snatched the book from her.

"Got it," she said. "Let's go, Abigail."

I was amazed. I thought she would have been crying by now. I almost was. But Sarah was absolutely calm, as if she hadn't heard a thing they'd said. I could tell by how pale she was that she was very upset, but she wouldn't let Pamela see it. I thought she must be very brave.

"Yeah, let's go, Sarah." I put my arm right around her shoulders and we walked off together without even turning our heads to look at them. I knew that would drive Pam crazy. She hates to be ignored.

"Fine!" I heard her call after us. "Go off with your dorfball friend, Abby, but don't think you're an FBO member anymore."

"Pam!" said Kate. She sounded pretty surprised.

"Well, she's not, Kate," Pam said. "And if she thinks she's coming to my birthday party and meeting Denver James, she's out of her mind."

Then she stormed off in the other direction. Kate followed behind her.

Sarah and I didn't say anything to each other for a while. We just walked quietly together, and I kept my arm around her shoulder the whole way. Then when we were turning the corner toward our street, I heard her say something.

"What?" I said.

"I said, thanks, Abigail. For sticking up for me that way."

"Me? I'm the one who got you involved in this mess in the first place. They're my friends — I mean, they *were* my friends. They had no right to talk to you that way."

"Well, but they're right," Sarah said. "I do talk a lot."

"That's just because you have a lot of interesting things to say, Sarah."

"I guess so." She didn't sound too convinced. "I saved our story, though," she continued.

"Yeah, that was really smart," I said.

"Lord Ivo used that trick on the wicked Earl of Shropshire when he was holding the diamond tiara he had stolen from Lady Eleanor."

I knew she must be feeling better if she was talking about Lord Ivo.

"Well, you sure rescued us," I told her.

"Hey, that makes me a hero," Sarah said.

"Heroine."

"I'm sorry about Pamela's birthday party, though."

"Well, I guess that was the *coup de grâce*."

"Yeah," Sarah said. "If things get any worse today, you may end up in the electric chair after all."

We both laughed a little, but I don't think either of us felt very good.

"Do you want to come over to my house?" Sarah asked. "I have Oreo cookies. Double Stuf."

I thought about what I would be doing right then if I had never met Sarah. Probably sitting around Pamela's house, eating taco dip and watching *Your Life to Lead*. We'd be planning Pam's party, talking about what Pam would wear, and who Pam would invite. Then I looked at Sarah, and I remembered the way she'd said "chivalrous" to Al the museum guard, and the way she laughs in whoops, and tells wonderful stories, and is really, really interested in my drawings.

"I can't think of anything I'd rather do, kind friend," I said in the most Sarah-like language I could think of. After all, I like Double Stuf Oreo cookies almost as much as taco dip.

7

Sarah couldn't find the Double Stuf Oreo cookies, so we had to settle for chocolate-covered graham crackers, which wasn't exactly the same thing. We both tried really hard to be cheerful, but we weren't very successful. We didn't even want to work on our story, after Pam had trashed it. The only good thing that happened was that Sarah's brother's friend David came over. He really is very cute, and he and Simon played basketball in the backyard all afternoon while we watched out Sarah's window. I think Simon's awfully cute, too, even though Sarah says I'm "positively addle-brained," which means crazy, I think.

When I got back to my house, I felt kind of nauseated. I don't know if it was because of Pamela, or just because I ate so many chocolate-covered graham crackers. A little of both, probably. The thing is, I couldn't stop thinking about the FBO club, and how I'd known them all forever, and how I probably wouldn't ever be friends with them again. Partly it seemed like Pamela's fault, but I also started to think about how things had been kind of different with the FBO ever since school started this year.

Last year, the For Blondes Only club was in the fifth grade at Lowell Elementary. We used to walk down the street together on the way to school, arm in arm, wearing our FBO hats.

Everybody was happier then. Mrs. Tucker and Mr. Tucker were still together, and we used to go over to Kate's house every Wednesday and Mrs. Tucker would take us bowling or ice-skating. Pamela had this little red ice-skating skirt that made her look like a real figure skater. She and Kate kept trying to do figure eights, but they always looked more like eggs. Beth and I didn't like to skate so much. We liked to watch all the skaters while we sat in the restaurant and drank that fake hot chocolate that tastes like air. It's weird how if your mom makes that for you you think it's gross, but at a skating rink it tastes just right. Beth got to know the life stories of all of the waitresses. After a while they started giving us free refills. Afterward we'd always have dinner at my house. The FBO club makes fun of Paul's commercials, but I have to say that none of them would turn down a chicken 'n' sauce dinner.

On nice days, even in the fall and winter, we'd get Lucia to drive us over to the beach. It's nice on the beach in the winter because it's so quiet and private. We used to collect shells and go back to Pamela's to make things. Beth had this book, *One Hundred and One Crafts for Kids*, and it had a bunch of ideas for stuff you can make with shells. But all of us were really lousy at it except Kate. She made this pretty shell bracelet for her mom. The rest of us actually just ended up playing with Pam's mother's makeup.

It's not like anything really special happened, not anything as exciting as meeting Denver James — which I would never get to do, now — but we all just had a lot of fun being with each other.

But this year everything's been different. I moved to a new house, so we couldn't walk to school together even if we wanted to. And Kate's mother isn't taking us anywhere this year. Kate's sad all the time. Beth's all caught up in her acting. Even if I hadn't met Sarah, things wouldn't have been the same.

So I sat on our porch thinking about all this, and getting nauseated, and drinking ginger ale. It didn't help. It also didn't help that Michael chose that exact moment to leap out of the kitchen window, shouting, "Cowabunga," and knocking my ginger ale all over my favorite jeans.

"Michael, you little creep, I'm going to kill you!" I screamed, grabbing him by his Batman cape, pinning him down, and pinching him hard on his arm.

"Owwwwww!" he yelled. "Mo-om, Abby's hurting me!"

"Shut up, you little tattletale," I hissed, pulling his hair.

I don't know what got into me. I mean, Michael bugs me a lot, but I usually just ignore him, and basically he's a good kid. For some reason, though, I just couldn't stop myself. I pinched him again.

"Abigail Lauren Wagner, you come here this minute!" Mom yelled.

I let Michael go. He started crying, just a little too noisily, if you know what I mean. I went inside.

"What!" I said.

"Abby, I don't know what's going on with you, but I want you to go to your room right now, and don't you even look through your keyhole until I say so," Mom said. She was getting very pink in the face, which always means she's really mad.

"Fine," I said. I was really mad, too.

I went up to my room and changed into dry pants. Fighting with Michael hadn't made me feel better, but at least it had given me something else to think about. I lay there brooding for a long time, then I heard my mom knocking on the door.

"May I come in?" she asked.

"Okay."

"Abby, what's the matter with you lately? You've really upset your brother."

"Half-brother."

I knew that was pushing it. Mom likes to think of me and Michael as regular brother and sister, and I do, too, most of the time.

"Fine, half-brother," she said. "You know, I'd be happy to talk to you about whatever is upsetting you, but it's totally unfair to take it out on your family like this. I want you to think about that."

Then she left the room. She was right, of course. Just because things were terrible with the FBO club was no reason to take it out on Michael and Mom. But I didn't care. I just wanted everyone else to feel as rotten as I did.

After a long time I heard another knock on my door.

"Abber?" Paul called through the door. "Do you want any dinner?"

Paul always thinks that if you're feeling down, dinner will make you feel better. Especially if dinner includes sauce.

"No," I said.

"Well, could you do me a favor?" he asked.

"What?" All I needed was to do Paul a favor. He opened the door and stuck his head in. "Could you listen to my new commercial?"

He came barreling into the room without even waiting for an answer. I couldn't believe what he was wearing. He had on this purple Hawaiian shirt, and a big straw hat and shorts. He was carrying bongo drums and a big tape deck that had some kind of Caribbean music playing.

"Come on, Abby," he said. "Let's get into a calypso frame of mind."

He pulled me off the bed and started to dance around me, beating his drums and singing to the music:

> *"Tell de people, if you see 'em*
> *Texas Paul's gone*
> *Caribbean.*
> *It's de taste dat makes dem smile*
> *Texas Paul's Jamaican Style.*
> *Everybody sing!*
> *Tell de people*
> *It so nice*
> *Tell dem*
> *Buy Jamaican Spice."*

"Ta-da!" he said, lifting me up in the air and tossing me on my bed like he used to do when I was six. "What do you think?"

He looked so happy and proud of himself standing there in that silly outfit that, for some reason, I just burst into tears.

"Abber! Abber! Hey, I didn't mean to . . . Is the song that bad?" he asked, sounding really worried.

"No!" I said, laughing and crying at the same time.

That's one of the most annoying things about Paul. It's hard not to laugh when he's around.

"That's a relief," he said. Then he sat down on the bed and put his arms around me. I cried on his shoulder for about fifteen minutes. He just sat there without saying anything. That's the nicest thing about Paul. He doesn't always want to *talk* about everything all the time like my mom does when I'm feeling bad. He just lets me feel bad.

After I wiped my eyes, I decided I was a little hungry after all. So I went downstairs and apologized to Michael and had some Jamaican chicken. Then I took a bath and laid out my clothes for the morning and did my homework and tried to sleep.

On my way to school the next morning, I thought about how I would act when I saw the FBO club. I didn't think I could even be in the same room with them without feeling sick, but I didn't have much choice. Usually I rush to homeroom, but today I just stood around the lockers for a while, hoping the bell would ring before I saw any of them. I almost made it, but just before the bell, Beth came rushing around the corner to her locker. She didn't see me right away, because she was in such a rush, but then she turned around and said, "Hi, Abby."

I didn't say anything. I didn't know what to say. I didn't even know if she knew about Pamela and Kate and me fighting.

"Beth, come here," I heard Pamela shout at her, before I had a chance to think up something.

I could see Pam and Kate standing in front of our homeroom impatiently. Beth went walking over to them, expecting me to follow, I guess, but I just stood against the wall. I saw Pam look at me in a really mean way, and then put her arm around Beth and start talking in this fast, soft voice. I could just imagine what she was saying about me. After a minute the bell rang, and I had to go in the room. Pam and Beth and Kate were in our corner, talking. Beth looked over at me, but I just looked away. There was an empty seat by the window, so I sat there all alone. I was never so happy to see Miss Moritz in my whole life.

We had English first period, and I just sat there next to Ellen Wu again, feeling lonely. I was starting to get used to it. The nice thing was that Ellen and I walked together to our next class, social studies. I used to think she was kind of dorfy, the way she tossed her hair around and giggled all the time, but I guess she's pretty nice. We walked to all our classes together. It wasn't like being with the FBO club, but at least she kept smiling at me. That was more than Pam did the whole morning.

At lunch I avoided the FBO half of the cafeteria, and went looking for Sarah. I found her next to the Jell-O squares. It was great to see a friend.

"Are you keeping your chin up?" she asked, grabbing a handful of potato chips.

"I guess so."

"Well, I was up all night making wonderful plans for Annabella and Alexander. Would you like to hear about them?"

"Sure," I said.

I didn't tell her what I had been up all night thinking about. I thought it would make her feel kind of bad. So I got myself a sandwich and walked over to a table with her. I was really glad to have someone to eat with. On our way we saw Ellen Wu and her friend Peggy Phillips. They waved us over.

"Do you want to sit here?" Ellen offered.

Sarah and I looked at each other. It seemed sort of unfriendly to say that we would rather work on our story. Anyway, Ellen was turning out to be okay.

"Sure," I answered.

"How come you're not sitting with Pamela? I thought you guys were joined at the hip," Ellen said.

"I don't want to," I told her. "I think she's pretty snotty, to tell you the truth." Saying that made me feel a lot better. All day I had been imagining the things Pam was saying to Beth and Kate about me, so it was sort of nice to tell someone what I thought of *her*.

Just as we were sitting down, Mr. MacFadden

walked by. He saw me sitting there and smiled at me. "Abby, how's the knee feeling?" he asked as he went by.

This sent Ellen and Peggy into a major giggling fit.

"Fine, thanks," I said.

It was nice of Mr. MacFadden to remember my knee. I think that's why he's such a good teacher. He remembers things.

"Do you, hee hee hee hee, y'know, hee hee hee, like Mr. MacFadden?" Ellen asked me, trying hard to control her giggling.

"Well, I think he's very nice," said Sarah.

"Me, too," I said.

"But do you, y'know, think he's cute?" asked Ellen. She said that in a whisper.

"Yes," said Peggy, "we both think he's *sooo* gorgeous, hee hee hee hee hee."

Why is it that giggly girls always hang out together, I wondered.

"Well," Sarah whispered to them, "I have always felt that he was a very romantic figure." She was getting into the spirit of this whole thing already. Sarah can smell romance a mile away. "I think he must have suffered some tragedy in his youth," she said.

"Really!" said Ellen.

"Yes. I think he's probably running from his past, if you must know," Sarah told them.

Ellen and Peggy were completely into this idea

of Mr. MacFadden's secret past, I could tell.

"Oh!" said Peggy.

By the time we were finished with lunch, Sarah had thought up an entire life story for Mr. MacFadden that was very exciting. Born in Ireland of poor, but honest, parents, he escaped a phony horse-theft charge and came to America where, after a hard life on the streets, he was taken in by a beautiful, but strangely sad, woman. . . . It went on and on like that. Sarah must lie awake at night making this stuff up. I have to say I just can't look at Mr. MacFadden in quite the same way anymore.

After lunch I had gym class, and then Sarah and I met and walked home together. It wasn't so bad. When I got home my mom was playing the piano in the living room. She does that sometimes when she's upset. She only knows how to play one song, "Frosty the Snowman," so she plays it over and over again. It's pretty weird. I went to the door and watched her for a while.

"Mom?"

"Abby, you startled me," she said.

"Mom, I'm sorry about yesterday."

"I know, honey. Is everything okay?" She put out her arm, and I sat down next to her.

"Not really," I said.

"Do you want to talk about it?"

"Not really."

I sat there for a little while, then she kissed me

on the head, and went into the kitchen to make dinner. I spent the rest of the afternoon watching Batman cartoons with Michael.

So I got through the day, at least, and I figured I'd probably get through the next day and the next. It just felt like something was missing. Like one of my arms. I just hoped it wouldn't feel that way forever.

8

Mr. MacFadden had assigned a composition for English class the day before. The topic was "Every Cloud Has a Silver Lining . . . Or Does It?" Mr. MacFadden likes to give us assignments that make us "think about our world." Anyway, it made me start wondering if there was a silver lining in this whole horrible fight with the For Blondes Only club. At first I thought there wasn't. It'd been a week since any of them had talked to me, and even though I still felt angry about it, I was sad and lonely, too. But Mr. MacFadden had said we had to think long and hard about this, and not write the first thing that came into our heads. So after thinking long and hard, I came up with a little bit of silver.

First of all, there was Sarah. I guess my dream would have been to have all of us be friends again. But if I couldn't have that, I was glad I made a great friend like Sarah out of this whole mess. We walked back and forth to school every day together, and ate lunch together, too. It's made being without the FBO club a little bit easier.

Second of all, I suppose, was that I found out it's not that hard to make new friends. I'd always stuck pretty much with the FBO club, but now that I couldn't, I started to make friends with Ellen Wu and Peggy Phillips, and they turned out to be fun. It wasn't the same as having the FBO club, but it felt good to know that people like me even when I'm not part of the club.

Sarah's class had a different assignment. She told me about it when we walked to school that morning. They had to write about "What makes you afraid?" Sarah wrote a story with a bunch of ghosts and dripping blood in it. I wasn't sure if that's what Mr. MacFadden had in mind. I told her how much I liked it, though. And I did, too. That's the thing about Sarah — she can make a great story out of anything.

After I waved good-bye to her, I went into my homeroom. There was a big sign on the blackboard:

DANCE COMMITTEE ELECTIONS TOMORROW

I'd completely forgotten about the Thanksgiving Dance. I couldn't believe it was such a short time ago that Pamela had suggested I run for the dance committee. It seemed like a million years. But the more I thought about it, the more I thought, "Why not run?" Just because Pam and I weren't friends anymore didn't mean it wasn't a good idea. Mostly what the committee did was choose a theme and plan decorations, which I would be pretty good at. Usually I don't like to run for things. Pam and Beth had been president and vice-president of the fifth grade, and Kate was once elected "Christmas Elf," I think because she sort of looks like an elf. But I never like to run for things, because you have to get up in front of people and talk.

The dance committee was different, though. For one thing, I didn't think anyone would even run against me. Mary Kosinski and Lauren Glaser, who always get elected to things, were already president and treasurer of the class. I didn't think any of the *boys* would be interested in planning a dance. Ashley Landers, who's in Ms. Baker's class with Sarah, would probably run, because she runs for everything, but nobody ever votes for her because she's sort of dorfy and she always makes these terrible speeches about good citizenship. I think her mother writes them.

So, I thought, why not? I was trying to do things that were fun without the FBO club, and this would be a good way to start. I was so lost in thought that I didn't even notice the club in their corner. Until then, even though I tried to ignore them, I could always hear them whispering and talking in the back of the room. Maybe I was finally learning to live without them. By the time

Miss Moritz came in, I had decided to run.

"Class, you may have noticed that the Thanksgiving Dance is just around the corner, and we need a chairperson for the dance committee," Miss Moritz said.

The girls all giggled a little at this, but the boys looked kind of gloomy. I don't think there would be a Thanksgiving Dance if it were up to them.

"If anyone is interested in running, please raise your hand," Miss Moritz continued.

I was going to raise my hand, but I felt kind of nervous about it.

"Nobody at all?" Miss Moritz asked. "Class, I'm very disappointed in your lack of school spirit."

It was now or never. I raised my hand.

"Abigail Wagner," Miss Moritz said. "Very good, Abigail. I will inform Ms. Baker's class, and we'll hold the elections tomorrow. I'm sure *many* of them have expressed interest."

Miss Moritz always tries to make us feel like Ms. Baker's homeroom is the better class, but I was sure no one but Ashley had decided to run. Then I heard a voice from the back of the room. It was Pamela's voice.

"I'll run, too, Miss Moritz. I think dance committee would be fun."

I looked over at her. I couldn't believe she was doing this. I knew it was just to get back at me. I mean, it had been her idea for me to run in the first place. I should have known something like this would happen. Now I was stuck running against Pamela. All the girls would vote for her because she was popular and gave these great parties and knew Denver James. All the boys would vote for her because she was the most beautiful girl in school. I would look like a complete idiot. And Pamela would just love that. I felt like crying all over again. I guess I wasn't over the club as much as I'd thought.

"Don't fret so much, Abigail," Sarah said to me at lunch when I told her about it. "Everybody won't vote for Pam just because she's beautiful. I'm sure they will see that you have far more inner beauty."

"Well, maybe. But I'm not sure that 'inner beauty' is exactly what people look for in a dance committee chairperson."

"Perhaps not," Sarah said thoughtfully. "However, I'm sure if they knew about how talented you are, they would vote for you in an instant." She looked very thoughtful for a minute. "I have a marvelous idea! Tonight we will go through your sketchbook and pick out all the best pictures, and then tomorrow at the assembly you can display them. I'm sure everyone will be terribly impressed."

"Terribly impressed with what?" I heard Ellen say as she and Peggy sat down with us.

They had started eating lunch with us every day. Sarah would always have a new installment of the Mr. MacFadden story for them. In the last episode, he had been chased into a dark alley by the mobster husband of the poor showgirl who he loved from afar. I would have been terribly worried about him if I hadn't known for sure that he'd end up teaching English in a middle school in Connecticut. The mobster's name was Harry "the Knife," and he always carried a long Egyptian dagger with the initials of his victims carved in the side.

"With Abigail's drawings. She's going to show them at assembly tomorrow when she runs for dance committee," Sarah said.

"No, I'm not, Sarah."

"Why not, Abby? It would be awesome," Ellen said.

"I just don't want to show my drawings to the whole world," I told her.

"Okeydokey," said Ellen. "I hear Mr. Mac-Fadden is going to act as chaperone! Isn't that too totally wild?"

"Maybe he'll ask you to dance," I said.

That sent Ellen and Peggy into a fit of giggles. I thought they were going to choke.

"Anyway," I said to Sarah, "I'm going to just drop out of the whole election. What's the point of running if you can't win?"

I felt very hot and tired and sad, and I just wanted to splash some water on my face. It's not like being the head of the dance committee had been a lifelong dream or anything, but it made me feel lousy that Pam would go out of her way to keep me from doing it. So before Sarah could say anything, I got up from the table and went into the girls' bathroom.

As I opened the door, I saw Pam and Kate standing by the sink and trying on lipstick. "What do *you* want?" Pam said as she looked up and saw me.

"I just wanted to wash my hands, Pamela."

I couldn't believe it. It's hard when you can't even use the bathroom in peace at your own school.

Pam looked at Kate, but Kate just turned away from both of us, like she didn't want to be involved. Pam seemed a little mad when she did that. I was kind of surprised myself.

"Well, don't bother us, okay?" Pam said. "And don't bother showing up for assembly tomorrow, either, because there's no way you can beat me."

"I'll be there," I said. She'd made me so angry, I wasn't going to quit now for all the taco dip in Mexico.

"Fine," said Pam, and she took Kate's arm and walked out of the room.

I stood in the bathroom for a minute, trying to pull myself together. School used to be sort of boring, but it was getting to be just one crisis after another. I liked boring better. After I splashed some cold water on my face and brushed my hair, I felt a little better. Then I heard the door open again.

"Abigail?" Sarah said, peeking her head in the door.

"Hi, Sarah."

"Abigail, I wish to apologize for my impropriety at the luncheon table."

"What does that mean in English?" I asked kind of nastily.

"It means, I'm sorry for what I said. About your drawings. I know you don't like to show them to people. I just think they're so marvelous — "

"Well, I've decided you're right," I said, cutting her off. "If that's what it takes to beat Pamela, then I'll do it."

"Splendid, Abigail, that's the spirit! Would you like me to help you write your speech?"

"Sarah, from now until tomorrow afternoon, I am all yours. Let's get to work."

That evening Sarah came over to my house and we worked on my speech. First we wrote it, and then we practiced my "presentation" until Sarah thought I sounded perfect. Then we went through my sketchbook and picked out all the best drawings, to show people that I had "the necessary artistic spirit," as Sarah put it. Then we tried the speech out on my mother and Paul. Then we went over to Sarah's house and tried the speech out on *her* mother. I practiced it for the rest of the night. While I did my homework. While I took a bath.

While I brushed my teeth. By the time I was ready for bed, I knew I could get up in front of everybody. Pam might win the election, but it wouldn't be because I gave in!

As we all filed into the auditorium the next day, I could feel my stomach getting nervous. I just wanted to say my speech and show my pictures and run. But first we had to sit through all the announcements about the Drama Club rehearsal, and football practice, and not throwing soda cans out with the rest of the trash. We had to applaud the Debating Club for their great victory over Carson Middle School. We had to hear about the annual Thanksgiving food drive. I just kept getting more and more butterflies. Finally it was time for our election speeches. Of course we were going in alphabetical order. Why does everything always have to be in alphabetical order? Why does my last name have to start with W? The butterflies were turning into bats.

Pam got up to make her speech. She was dressed in a red and white striped dress that would have made me look like a barber pole, but it made her look really cute. Her hair was pulled up into a braid and it had red bows in it, going all the way down her back. Sometimes Pam dresses to look sort of sophisticated, and I think some of the kids are a little afraid of her. Today she looked great, but just like the girl next door. I had to admit it, Pam always picked exactly the right thing to wear.

She got up on the stage and turned around and gave her best smile. "Hi, everybody!" she said, waving. "I know you'll all vote for me 'cause you want to go and have fun at the dance, and I can tell you, I know how to make a dance really fun!"

She was so perky, you wanted to barf, but I could tell everyone thought she was adorable. Even the teachers had these goofy smiles as they looked at her. That's the thing about being beautiful. You can say the stupidest things and you'll still have everyone slobbering all over you. She went on for a while about how she always gave great parties. When she sat down, everyone clapped.

Then Ashley went up to make her speech. She was so freaked out to be following Pam that you couldn't hear a word she said. I felt pretty sorry for her, actually. But I have to admit, I was glad I didn't have to worry about her beating me, too. She hardly got any applause at all.

Finally it was my turn. I would never look as great as Pam, but I did have on my best-fitting jeans, and my mom had let me borrow her black sweater with the roses embroidered on it, and helped me fix my hair so it actually fell into place instead of in my face.

I walked up the aisle to the stage, and I could hear my heart beating with every step. When I got there, I turned around and looked out at all of the kids in the whole school. And my mind went completely blank. The speech that Sarah and I had worked on so hard, the speech that I could say in my sleep, the speech that was my only chance of beating Pam in the election, was completely gone. I had nothing to say. Desperately I looked out at the audience. They were all watching me, expecting something. I didn't know what to do. I was just about to run away, embarrassed and humiliated forever, when I spotted Sarah in the fifth row. She was smiling her best smile at me. I couldn't let her down after all the work she'd done.

So I took a deep breath, and I smiled, and, without for one single second taking my eyes off Sarah's face, I began. "My fellow students, the job of dance committee chairperson is a very important job. She is responsible for all of the decorations and posters, and also for the music and refreshments. You may not know that I have a lot of interest in painting and drawing, and I think I could be very good at decorating the gym and making posters. Also, my stepfather makes Texas Paul's Bar-B-Que Sauce, and he has already agreed to provide barbequed wings for the refreshments."

I didn't mention that he would be doing that no matter who was in charge of the dance committee.

"I have some of my drawings here, if you are interested."

I pulled the drawings out of my bag. The people in the back couldn't see them at all, but the ones in the front sort of sighed. I hoped that was good. What if they hated all the drawings? The butterflies were starting their somersaults in my stomach again. Then I looked at Sarah. She was giving me the thumbs-up sign. The butterflies went away.

"In conclusion, I want to say that as chairperson I will do my best to see that we all have a good time. Thank you for listening."

I just wanted to get off that stage as fast as I could. But I had remembered most of the speech, and even if I didn't beat Pamela, I was glad I hadn't quit. I rushed down the aisle, trying to look dignified and run at the same time. It wasn't until I got to my seat that I realized everyone was applauding for me, almost as much as they did for Pam. Maybe I had a chance of winning this thing after all.

They would announce the winners at the end of our lunch period. I was so nervous, I didn't want to eat, so I just stood around outside the cafeteria, waiting to hear the announcement. I was just standing there, biting my fingernails, when someone said to me:

"Yo, Abby. Don't bite your hand off."

It was Josh Baron. He isn't the cutest boy in school, but he is the cutest in our homeroom. He has blond hair and freckles and these very, very long eyelashes. I don't know why it is, but boys always seem to have the longest eyelashes. He had never said one single word to me before in his life, and he's been in my class since fourth grade.

"What?" I asked.

"I said, don't bite 'em off. You've got nothing to worry about. I had all my friends vote for you."

"You did?" I couldn't imagine why.

"Yeah," he said.

I smiled. I didn't know what to say. I'd never really talked to a boy who wasn't my brother.

"So."

"So."

"So, good luck."

"Thanks," I told him.

He smiled at me, a very cute smile, and walked off. I was so shocked, I didn't even care if I won anymore. Josh Baron! Sarah would never believe it. I was rushing over to tell her when Miss Moritz got up and raised her hand for quiet. The winners were about to be announced.

"Everybody, the votes have been counted, and your new dance committee chairwomen are . . ."

Are? I thought.

"Pamela Baldwin and Abby Wagner. It's a tie! Congratulations to both of you."

A tie. I couldn't believe it. That was worse than losing. That was worse than anything.

9

"I had the weirdest dream last night," I said to Sarah. We were on our way to the auditorium for the first Thanksgiving Dance committee meeting. I had wanted to tell her about the dream all day. It had really been bothering me.

"Do tell," Sarah said, munching a sugar doughnut she must have stuck in her pocket at lunch. "I'm excellent at dreams."

"Well, Pamela and I were in this big lake, and all of a sudden these huge turkeys started coming up from under the water."

"Immense swimming turkeys," said Sarah. "How gruesome."

"The grossest part is that they all had their heads cut off," I told her.

"Ghastly."

"Then they started to claw at my legs and try to pull me under the water. And Pamela was laughing and pointing. Then I think I screamed or something. And then I woke up." I looked at Sarah to see what she thought.

"Well," said Sarah, licking the sugar off her fingers thoughtfully, "your dream is less mysterious than it may seem."

"It is?"

"Indeed," Sarah said. "Just think about it. Turkeys, Pamela, beheadings, screaming. You had the dream because you're worried about seeing Pamela at the dance committee meeting."

That made sense. I certainly was worried. I'd been thinking about the stupid dance committee ever since the election, trying to figure out how to make the best of a rotten situation. I mean, there was no point in doing a lousy job just because I had to work with Pam. I really wanted the dance to look good so that all the kids would be glad they'd voted for me. Even dealing with Pamela was better than having the whole entire school think I was an idiot.

"I guess I could have figured that dream out for myself," I said, feeling a little foolish about having such an unmysterious dream.

"Of course, it could mean that you want to become a vegetarian," Sarah said. "But that seems less likely."

We had reached the auditorium doors. I wondered if Pamela and the girls were already inside. We were each allowed to pick our own staff. I'd picked Sarah. Pamela, of course, would have picked Beth and Kate. I must have gone pale or something because Sarah took one look at me and grabbed hold of my arm.

"Be brave, Abigail," she said. "Hold your head high. As Lord Ivo would say, 'Once you know your enemy, he is forever yours.'"

I wasn't sure what that meant, but it made me feel a little better. Not that I *wanted* the FBO club to be my enemies. It just seemed to be the way things had turned out. I held my head as high as I could, and Sarah and I walked into the auditorium.

Pamela, Kate, and Beth were already there. As soon as Sarah and I came in, they stopped talking to each other and just sat and stared at us. Pamela was staring in an extremely nasty way. Sarah and I had to walk across the whole auditorium floor in complete silence. It was kind of nerve-racking. I looked over at Sarah, but her head was so high, I could only see her chin.

When we got to the table where the girls were sitting, Pamela looked us over as if we were wearing garbage bags or something, and then turned to Beth and Kate and said in a very obnoxious way, "Well, look who's here."

"Hi, Pam," I said. "Hi, Beth. Hi, Kate." I was sort of hoping that the FBO club had decided they didn't want to look like idiots in front of the whole school, either.

"Greetings, all," Sarah said. I could tell the girls wanted to burst out laughing at that one. I knew Sarah was nervous, but I couldn't help wishing that she would be more normal, just for a few minutes.

"So," I said, trying to act like everything was fine. "Have you guys made any important decisions?"

"Just one," said Pamela. "We decided that there are too many people on the dance committee. You know, five's a crowd."

She glanced over at Kate the way she always did when she wanted Kate to agree with her, but Kate didn't even look up. I noticed that Kate looked particularly thin and tired.

"Oh, stop it, Pam," Beth said. She looked at all of us around the table. I smiled at her, but she didn't smile back. "Listen, everybody, we have work to do. And we don't have time to sit around having a fight. Now, I've made up a list of the stuff we should talk about today."

Beth pulled out a page from her notebook. Even if she wouldn't smile at me, I was glad she was there. At least she was willing to work together. Besides, I missed her.

"Theme, decorations, music, food, chaperones," Beth read from her list. "Can anyone think of anything else?"

No one said a word.

"Okay, then," Beth said. "Let's decide on a theme." She looked at her watch. "I have rehearsal in an hour."

"The theme is pretty obvious, Beth," Pamela said. "I mean, it's the Thanksgiving Dance, right?"

"Yeah," Beth said, "but that doesn't mean we have to decorate the place with turkeys, does it?"

"No," I said quickly. "Maybe we could make autumn our theme. We could hang lots of gold and red crepe paper, and make leaves out of oak tag and hang them all around. We could even make some big trees out of papier-mâché." I had thought this up last night.

"Sounds pretty," said Beth, which made me feel good. This meeting wasn't turning out so bad after all.

"Pretty *stupid*," said Pamela.

Though things could definitely get worse.

Kate only sighed.

"I have an idea," Sarah said. "Why don't we get everyone in the class to write about something that they're thankful for?"

"Oh, great," Pamela said sarcastically. "Then we can hang all the pieces of paper from Abby's trees. Or even better," she went on obnoxiously, "why don't we decorate the trees with some of your very moving poetry?"

Sarah looked down at the floor.

"Do you think maybe you could drop the poetry

bit, Pam?" I said. "It's getting old."

Pam opened her mouth, but Kate interrupted before she could talk. "It's sick that you guys can't go five minutes without fighting," she said. "I'm getting really tired of fighting."

"Pardon us, Kate. We didn't know you were so sensitive," Pamela snarled.

Everybody just sat there for a minute.

"How about if we forget about the theme for a while, and talk about the music," Beth suggested.

"Fine," I said.

The truth is that in spite of everything I'd told myself, I was starting to think this whole thing was a big mistake. It was pretty obvious we weren't going to be able to agree on anything, and I was just getting angrier and angrier at Pam. It was weird how much you could hate someone who you'd thought you really liked.

"First of all, we need to arrange with somebody to set up the sound system," said Beth. "And then I guess we'll all bring in our favorite tapes."

"Well," Pamela said, looking right at Sarah, "let's make sure it's cool music. We don't want any weird stuff." Then she flipped her hair over her shoulders and glared at me.

"Why don't we just show all the tapes to you so you can decide if they're cool enough, Pam," I said. "I mean, we all know what an expert you are."

"Who said I'm an expert, Abby?" Pam replied.

"You always act like one," I said.

"Shut up, you guys," said Kate, putting her hands over her ears. "Gosh, you sound like my parents."

"Well, if Pam could be a little less obnoxious for once in her life, maybe we could actually accomplish something here," I said, folding my hands on the table.

"*Me!*" Pam exclaimed. She was getting a little red in the face. "Why me? *I'm* not the one who dropped all her friends to hang around with some — "

"Excuse me, did you say that *I* dropped you?" I asked, cutting Pam off before she could say something else mean about Sarah. "I believe *you* were the one who stole our book and made fun of us and uninvited me to your precious birthday party."

"Yeah, well, *I'm* not the one who lied."

"What?" This sort of caught me off guard. "I don't know what you're talking about." Though, of course, I did.

"Hmm, let's see. Where shall I begin?" Pam said, tapping her forehead and crinkling her eyes like she was thinking very hard. "How about, 'My mom's *making* me go to the museum, I just can't get out of it.' Or, I know, 'We *had* to stop over at Granny Gargul's for dinner. . . .' "

"Okay, okay. I get the point, Pam."

"Do you?" Pam asked. "I'm not so sure. But I certainly don't want you to waste your valuable time worrying about *my* feelings. Not when you have your new little buddy here."

Pamela nodded her head in Sarah's direction.

"Yeah, well, maybe I wouldn't have had to lie if you'd given Sarah more of a chance," I stammered. I couldn't believe that my lies had finally caught up with me. I felt completely ashamed.

"Ha," said Beth. "You're one to talk about giving people chances."

"What's that supposed to mean?" I asked, surprised. I was so involved with Pamela, I'd almost forgotten Beth was there.

"It means that maybe you should have asked me how *I* felt before you decided we weren't friends anymore," said Beth. "I mean, when I leave for auditions, we're all sitting around talking about boys, and when I come back, we're enemies. Everybody's talking behind everybody else's backs. I can't even tell you about getting a part in the play." Beth's voice started to crack a little. "*I* didn't steal your book, Abby. *I* didn't uninvite you to anything. Gosh, we've been friends our whole lives."

I looked down at my folded hands. It made me feel bad to hear how upset Beth sounded. Still, she hadn't exactly made a huge effort to be friends with me lately.

"I didn't decide we weren't friends anymore," I said. "When you didn't talk to me, I just figured you took their side."

"Well, I was sort of hoping that you'd call me or something," Beth said.

"Yeah, well, maybe I was hoping that you'd call me, too," I said. I bit at my thumbnail for a minute. This was all very confusing. I wasn't sure what I was supposed to say, so I figured I'd just tell the truth. "I didn't ever really want to be in a fight with you, Beth," I said.

Beth smiled. "Me, either," she said. "I've missed you."

"*Beth!*" Pam exploded.

"And I'd love to see the book you and Mo — uh, you and Sarah are writing, if you ever want to show it to me," Beth went on, ignoring Pam completely.

"Beth!" Pam shouted. "How can you say that?"

"Oh, come on, Pam," said Beth. "Let's drop it already."

"Nice, Beth. Real nice," said Pamela, seething. "Now that you and Abby have done your little kiss-and-make-up bit, you're going to tell me what to do? But you know what?" she went on. "I don't have to take this from you. Because I know exactly why you're saying this. It's because you're all jealous of me."

My mouth fell open. But before I could say anything, Kate spoke up.

"Jealous of *you*!" she said. "We're jealous of you?"

"Of course," Pam said, with a flick of her hair, though I'm sure she was as shocked as the rest of us that Kate was talking back to her.

"You know, Pam," Kate said quietly, "I think you've got that wrong. The one who's jealous here is *you*."

Pam laughed nervously, but Kate took a deep breath and kept going. "You're jealous that people think Sarah's a better writer than you are," she said. "You're jealous that Abby has made other friends. You're jealous when *anybody* can do *anything* that you can't do. You'd better stop thinking that you're queen perfect all the time, because you're not. You're just a regular person, Pam. Like everyone else."

There was absolute silence when Kate finished talking. She was leaning on the table, breathing very hard, like she'd just run a race. Pam had turned the color of a tomato. For a minute I thought that she was going to cry. Usually Pam looks like she's in control of every situation, but now she just looked like a miserable little kid.

"Oh, yeah?" she sputtered.

It was amazing. For the first time in her whole life, Pam didn't know what to say.

"Look, Pam, I — " Kate started.

"You what, Kate?" Pam said. "You what? Maybe you ought to think about what you say to your closest friends, that is, if you expect to have any friends left."

"Oh, Pam!" said Beth.

But Pam just turned away. I heard Kate take a deep breath and saw the tears form in her big brown eyes. Then, without another word, she stood up, pushed her chair into the table so hard that the whole thing shook, and ran out of the room. We all sat there for a minute, sort of numb, not looking at each other. Then Beth stood up.

"Do you think I should try to find her?" she asked.

"Maybe she needs to be by herself for a little while," I said, hoping not to sound like a know-it-all.

"Gosh, what a mess," said Beth, sitting back down.

I looked over at Pam, but she had her head buried in her hands. Her hair had fallen all around her shoulders, so I could barely see her at all. I wondered what she was thinking.

"Well, I guess that's the end of the meeting," I said, sort of stupidly.

"Yeah, I guess," Beth said.

We sat quietly for another few minutes. I was hoping Kate would come back. I heard a couple of sniffles from Pam's direction, but she wouldn't look up.

"I hope Katie's okay," said Beth.

"I hope so, too," said Sarah.

There was another sniffle. "Me, too," said Pamela, softly, through her hair.

The bell rang to let us know that last period was over, but nobody even moved.

10

After a while, it was pretty obvious that Kate wasn't going to come back, and Beth had to go to rehearsal, so we each headed our separate way home. I wanted to ask Pamela to walk with Sarah and me, but she left so quickly that I didn't have a chance. She looked terrible when she left, and I felt sorry for her, even though I knew the whole thing was pretty much her own fault. It's hard for anyone to hear bad things about themselves and for Pam it's even harder. And while everything Kate said is true, it's also true that there are a lot of great things about Pam you sort of forget when she acts like such a jerk. She can always make you laugh, even if you're feeling really bad. She'd lend you her absolute fanciest dress if you had somewhere special to go. And, believe it or not, her friends are the most important thing in the world to her, even though she may have a weird way of showing it.

As Sarah and I walked home, I was thinking about Pam and Kate and Beth and everything that had gone on with the FBO club. I didn't feel much like talking, and to be honest, I didn't think that much about how Sarah might have been feeling. She'd been real quiet since we left school, and I knew that some mean things had been said about her at the meeting, but I sort of felt that the whole stupid mess was my problem, until she suddenly spoke.

"Oh, Abigail," Sarah said in a wavery, close-to-crying type of voice. "You must rue the day you ever met me."

"What?" I said, coming out of my own thoughts. I was very surprised at how sad she sounded. " . . . I don't rue it at all," I stammered, hoping I didn't sound like an idiot. I had absolutely no idea what "rue" meant.

"There is no need to spare my feelings," Sarah went on. "It is abundantly clear that I am the one who tore your lives asunder."

"The one who what?" Even though we'd been friends for a while now, I still sometimes felt as if Sarah spoke in another language.

"The one who destroyed the For Blondes Only club," she said mournfully. "I wouldn't blame you if you didn't want to be my friend anymore." Sarah shook her head and stuffed her hands into her pockets. I'd never seen her look so down. It made me feel doubly horrible that Sarah felt so hurt from all this FBO stuff, when really all she had ever been was a true-blue pal.

"Don't be such a dorf, Sarah," I said, putting my arm around her shoulders. "Of course I want to be your friend. You're the most unusual and talented person I know." She was, too.

"Unusual?" she asked nervously. "Or just strange?"

"Unusual, Sarah. You know, like there's nobody else like you." I wasn't sure if I was making her feel better or worse. "I think it's great."

Sarah smiled. I guess I'd said the right thing.

"I'm so glad we're friends, Abigail," she said, sounding much cheerier. "Let's go get some ice cream."

It's amazing how a triple-dip cone with sprinkles makes everything seem better. By the time we got to Big Bottom Road, we had stopped thinking about the meeting altogether and were deciding about what type of jewels Alexander would give to Annabella as a token of their love. I was imagining a gold and emerald tiara when my brother Michael appeared out of nowhere.

"Hey, Abs, you'd better move it," he said, pedaling his bicycle in circles around us. "Paul's commercial is going to be on any minute!"

"Oh, my gosh, I forgot," I said, starting to run home behind Michael's bike. "Come on, Sarah. Hurry!!"

Paul's new Jamaican Spice commercial was supposed to make its debut on the local five o'clock news that night. Texas Paul's sauce was one of the regular sponsors. I couldn't believe I'd almost missed it. I mean, even if the commercials are totally dorfed out, I still love Paul.

Mom was already sitting in front of the TV when Michael, Sarah, and I ran in. Paul was in the kitchen.

"We're here," I panted. "Sorry."

"Don't worry, you haven't missed anything," Mom said. "Hello, Sarah."

"Good afternoon, Mrs. Gargul," Sarah said.

"How did the meeting go, girls?" Mom asked.

I started to make a face and tell her, but Paul came bounding out of the kitchen. He was wearing his Hawaiian shirt and straw hat from the commercial, and carrying a huge platter of ribs 'n' sauce.

"A most gracious welcome to de beautiful ladies," he said in his terrible Jamaican accent and offered us some ribs.

Even though my stomach was full to the brim with ice cream, I took a couple so I wouldn't hurt Paul's feelings. Sarah took about fifty.

"Oh, oh, look! Here it is. Here it is." Mom was pointing to the TV and getting very excited.

"Turn it up," said Michael.

"Move your head," I said.

"Okay, everyone," said Paul, focusing on the television, "shhh."

I was totally shocked, but I had to admit, the commercial was actually sort of cute. I mean, Paul looked more funny than stupid, and the song was really kind of catchy. In fact, by the time they had run the commercial twice, we were all singing along. Paul sang the verse, and Sarah, Michael, and I sang the backup part that went, "Tastes so nice, nice, nice. Jamaican Spice, spice, spice." Mom shook her coin purse to make it sound like steel drums.

The whole thing was a lot of fun, and we were all laughing and congratulating Paul when the phone rang. Mom answered it, giggling, but right away her expression changed. "Why, no, Nan," I heard Mom say. "She's not over here. Let me ask Abby if she knows anything."

Mom put her hand over the receiver and turned to me. She almost didn't have to say a word. I knew right away what had happened. Nan was Kate's mother's name.

"Abs," Mom said. "This is Mrs. Tucker. Kate hasn't come home tonight. Do you have any idea where she might be?"

My stomach jumped into my throat. Suddenly, I felt like I had done something terribly wrong. I looked over at Sarah, who had guilt written all over her face.

"She got sort of upset in the meeting this afternoon," I said, hoping that I wouldn't have to tell the whole story.

"And," Mom said.

"And, well, she sort of ran out before it was over," I continued.

"No one has seen her since," Sarah finished for me, a little too dramatically.

"Oh, dear," said Mom, and turned back to the phone.

I sat down on the couch and bit my nails, the whole miserable dance committee meeting flashing before my eyes. I listened to Mom tell Kate's mother that she would call if she heard anything at all. Then she hung up the phone and looked very closely at Sarah and me.

"Girls," she said seriously, "is there something I should know?"

"Well," I said.

"Actually," said Sarah.

"I'm waiting," Mom said.

"It was just a big fight, Mom," I said. "A big, gigantic fight. Kate said some stuff, and Pam said some stuff, and then Kate started to cry and ran out."

I decided not to tell Mom about all the yelling the rest of us did. I didn't want her to think it was my fault, even though I felt as if it were.

"Can you think of any place where she might be?" Mom asked.

I shrugged my shoulders. I honestly had no idea

at all where Kate could have gone, especially now that it was getting dark and cold. I'd only run away once in my whole life, and I'd had to go to the bathroom so badly that I went back home before even getting to the next street.

But Sarah spoke up. "Yes, actually, Mrs. Gargul," she said confidently. "And if you'll let us, I believe that Abigail and I can find her."

"You do?" I asked.

Sarah kicked me in the shin.

"I mean, of course we can find her, Mom. Positutely."

I held my breath. I knew Mom wasn't going to let us go out looking for Kate. Not with the sun already down.

"It's six o'clock," Sarah said. "I promise we will have Kate back by seven."

Sarah seemed so sure of this. I wondered what she knew that I didn't. Mom glanced out the window and nibbled at her lower lip.

"Okay, girls," Mom said finally. "But I want you back here at seven o'clock, Kate or no Kate. Understand?"

"Yes, Mom."

"An hour is all we'll need," said Sarah. "And a flashlight. Now, let's synchronize our watches."

Five minutes later, Sarah and I were hurrying down Big Bottom Road, pulling our jackets around us. I felt like we were foreign spies on a top-secret mission. Even though I was worried about Kate, it was sort of exciting.

"Hey, Sarah, where are we going?"

"Shhhh," Sarah whispered, glancing around us to make sure no one would hear. "To the beach, of course."

"The beach!?"

For a second, I thought she might have been talking in some foreign spy code or something. I mean, nobody would be hanging around the beach alone when it was so cold and dark outside. But Sarah put her finger to her lips and nodded.

"I don't really think we're going to find her there, Sarah."

"Abigail," said Sarah, walking so quickly that I had to take little skipping steps to keep up with her. "When the Countess of Broxbury was shunned by her beloved Cuthbert, she went to the beach to weep."

"Yes, but — "

"And when Harold of Kent discovered that he had accidently slain his brother in a duel for the hand of the fair Katerina, he went to the beach to ponder his fate."

"Yes, okay, but — "

"Lord Ivo himself has said that the best place to contemplate one's life is by the water's edge," Sarah said. "Now, hurry. We don't have much time."

"But Sarah — " I couldn't believe this. I mean, maybe for Lord Ivo's crowd, the beach was a cool place to go, but I knew Kate, and there was no way.

"Quit dawdling, Abigail," said Sarah, hurrying ahead of me. "We're wasting time."

I wondered how she planned to get us all the way to the beach and back by seven o'clock.

"You know, Sarah. The beach is miles from here."

"I know a shortcut through Miller's Woods. We can get there in fifteen minutes."

I felt a chill go through me, and it wasn't just the wind. I know it's babyish, but I'm petrified of the woods at night. All those huge shadowy trees, and dark places you can barely see. Not to mention bats. And then there was that story Paul told about the dozens of arms and legs they found buried there. He swore it was true.

"Uh, Sarah," I called in a whisper. She had gotten pretty far ahead of me. "SARAH!"

"What *is* it, Abigail?" she said. I could tell she was getting impatient with me.

"Well, I, uh . . ." I started, but then I stopped. I couldn't say I was too chicken to go. Not when Sarah was willing to do all this. I mean, it was *my* friend we were searching for, even if we were searching for her in the most ridiculous place.

"Wait for me," I said, running to catch up with her.

We ran the rest of the way to Miller's Woods, and were huffing and puffing when we got there.

I tried to convince myself that it was no big deal to just march right on in, but the woods looked so scary when we got there that I told Sarah I had to get a pebble out of my shoe, and I sat down on the grassy hill to try and get my courage up. I was shaking the imaginary stone out of my sneaker when we heard a noise.

"What was that?" I asked, practically jumping out of my skin.

"I don't know."

We held our breath for a minute, frozen. Then it came again.

"It sounds like voices," Sarah said.

Voices. Probably the voices of some escaped prisoners who roam the woods looking for limbs to bury.

"Oh, gosh, Sarah," I said, taking her arm. "I knew we shouldn't have come. Let's get out of here."

Then through the trees came a blinding light.

"Come on!" I said. "They'll cut us to pieces and bury our arms."

I lifted my sneaker over my head, ready to hurl it at our attackers.

"No one is going to cut us to pieces, Abigail. And we must think of poor Kate." Then she called out into the darkness. "Who goes there?"

I heard the rustling of leaves and waited, terrified, as the light got closer and closer.

"Who goes there, I say!" Sarah called out again.

I couldn't believe how brave Sarah was. I bet even Lord Ivo wasn't this brave. I closed my eyes and crossed my fingers and prayed that we weren't going to end up armless. A voice shouted out from behind the light.

"Abby? Sarah? Is that you?"

I opened my eyes. Was it possible?

"Beth?"

Sure enough, there was Beth, bundled up in her down jacket, hurrying toward us. Behind her, kicking at the ground as she walked, was Pamela.

I looked up at Sarah. "Well, this ought to be interesting," I said.

Sarah shrugged.

"What are you guys doing here?" asked Beth. Her cheeks were very pink from the cold.

"Looking for Kate," I replied. It seemed like a pretty stupid answer from someone sitting on the ground, shaking a sneaker.

"You're kidding," Beth said.

"No," I said, standing up and sounding a little annoyed. "Sarah thought she might be at the beach. We were cutting through."

Beth looked at me, amazed.

"I told you so," said Pamela.

"I can't believe it," Beth said.

"I told you so," Pam said again.

"What?" I said. I felt very uncomfortable having Pam there. Escaped prisoners would have been easier to deal with.

"Pam thinks that Kate's at the beach, too," said Beth. "Personally, I think it's stupid. Why anyone would sit outside in the freezing cold — "

"Oh, Beth," Pam said, exasperated. "You just don't understand. I mean, where did Monica go when Denver James told her that her mother had been found in the psycho ward? Where did old Mrs. Porter go when she found out that Brice was really her kidnapped son?"

"Where did Ashley hide when Dr. Grant Hanover was trying to have her poisoned?" said Sarah.

"What?" I said.

My mouth must have dropped open. Of all the strange things that had happened that day, Sarah knowing about Dr. Hanover trying to poison Ashley seemed like the strangest. When did Sarah ever watch *Your Life to Lead*? I could tell Pam and Beth were completely surprised, too.

"You watch *Your Life to Lead*?" Pam asked Sarah. It was the first time she had even acknowledged that there was anybody else in the woods besides her and Beth. I guess she felt uncomfortable with me there, too.

"Only recently," said Sarah. "Since Abigail enjoys it so."

This was news to me, but Sarah acted as if it were the most normal thing in the world, so I didn't say anything.

"Well, then," said Pam to Beth. She still wouldn't look directly at me. "You see that Sarah understands completely. The beach is the perfect place to go when you're extremely bummed."

"Indeed," said Sarah. "That's exactly what I've been trying to tell Abigail."

"Well, I think Beth's just scared of the woods," Pam continued to Sarah. "She thought you guys were ax murderers."

"Abigail thought you were going to cut off our arms," Sarah said. I was amazed at how nice she and Pam were being to each other. It sounded as if they had been friends their whole lives.

"No!" Pam said in disbelief.

Sarah nodded.

Beth and I looked at each other.

"I thought you might cut off our legs, too," I added, figuring I might as well get into the conversation.

"Actually, I've been looking for a couple of nice ears to add to the collection," Beth said, starting to laugh.

"And a nose with freckles," Pam said shyly. I knew that she meant mine. I smiled at her, which I think made her feel better. "We thought maybe we could borrow your ax," she continued.

"I'll get it for you," said Sarah with a whoop. "Let me just wipe the blood off first."

"No, leave the blood on," said Pam.

"Yeah, we're thirsty," Beth added.

"Oh, yuck!" I screamed.

If there were any escaped ax murderers hanging around, they must have thought we were pretty strange ourselves, standing there in the cold, grossing ourselves out and laughing. It felt really good to laugh with Pam and Beth again. For a minute, I think we'd all forgotten why we were there, but then Sarah looked at her watch.

"Oh, no," she said. "Seven o'clock draws nigh. We'll have to hurry if we want to find Kate."

"Well, come on, let's go," Pamela said. Then she turned to Beth and me. "Unless you two want to wait here," she said with a glance at Sarah. "I'm sure Sarah and I can find her."

"No, no. We'll come," I said, pulling Beth along with me. "We're not the wimps you think we are."

"Oh, yes, you are," Pam said. "But that's okay." Then she smiled. "Hey, I have an idea," she went on. "Maybe Sarah can write a song for you guys to sing. You know, to keep your spirits up."

"A song?!" I said. I knew I shouldn't have opened my mouth. I mean, I guess this was Pamela's way of apologizing, but I was so utterly shocked by everything that was going on that I couldn't help it.

"Well, okay," said Sarah to Pam. "How about . . . stay away, bad guys. Do me no harm."

Then Pam chimed in.

"I want to keep my legs and arms."

The two of them thought this was the funniest

thing they had ever heard. Nobody but me noticed that something was coming toward us down the road.

"Uh, you, you guys," I stuttered, pointing.

But even Beth was busy singing.

"You guys," I said again, tugging on Beth's sleeve.

"What is it? . . . Oh, my goodness," Beth said, tugging on Pamela's arm.

"Well, now we're dead ducks," I said, wondering just how hard it would be to outrun an escaped prisoner.

"No, wait a second," Pamela said. "I think that's Kate."

"What? No."

"Is it?"

"Oh, my gosh, you're right. Hey, Kate!"

"KATE!"

"Katie, hey!"

We were all calling at once and rushing toward the skinny little figure that was walking down the dark road. In the glare of our flashlights, I could see Kate's smile.

"What are you doing?" she asked as we all gathered around her. "What are you all doing here?"

We didn't even answer, we were so happy to see her. Pam hugged her, and Beth hugged her, and I hugged her, and all three of us hugged her, and then, realizing that Sarah was just sort of standing there, I pulled her into the circle, and we all stood there hugging and laughing, and I felt a little like I might cry.

"You guys, this is crazy," Kate was saying, but I could tell she was really glad to see us, too.

"Where were you?" I asked.

"Everyone was so worried," said Beth.

"Me especially," said Pam.

"I went to the movies," Kate said. "Double feature. Then I got some hot chocolate and figured I'd come home. I'm sorry you worried." She smiled at us all.

"I'm sorry I said what I said, Katie," Pamela said.

"It's okay," Kate said. "I think I sort of overreacted."

"No," Pam said. "You were right. I was wrong." Then she turned to Sarah and me. "I was wrong about a lot of things," she continued. "Sometimes I can be a total idiot."

"Not a total idiot," said Sarah.

"Just a partial idiot," I said.

Pam put her arms around Kate and me.

"I love you guys," she said. "Now don't make me tell you again."

So at five minutes to seven, we headed back home, the five of us walking arm in arm, talking and giggling and chattering our teeth. Sarah started singing, "Stay away bad guys, do me no harm . . . ," and soon the rest of us were singing it, too, shouting at the tops of our lungs.

When we got to Honey Hollow Road, we all gave each other hugs good-bye, and Pam, Beth, and Kate headed off together.

"Hey, you guys," Pam called out over her shoulder. "Don't forget my party's this Saturday. I'd like you *both* to come. And I expect great presents."

"In your dreams, Pam," I called after her.

She stuck her tongue out at me, and I stuck mine out in return. I felt unbelievably happy.

My feet were frozen, my face was numb, and my ears hurt from the cold. Sarah and I hooked arms and put our heads down against the wind.

"I want to keep my legs and arms," we sang, practically dancing the rest of the way home.

144

11

The morning of Pam's birthday party I woke up before it was light. I couldn't believe I was actually going to meet Denver James in person. I was kind of nervous about it, too, I have to admit. I kept thinking about every way that I could embarrass myself. My palms could get all sweaty and gross when he went to shake my hand. A giant pimple could break out right on my nose. I could start giggling. I could sneeze right in his face. I could have something green caught between my teeth and not know it. The possibilities seemed endless.

Mostly I was just excited and happy, though.

"It's just amazing," I had said to Sarah on our way home from school yesterday. "If you'd told me a week ago that we would all be going to the party together, I never would have believed you."

"Miraculous things happen all the time, Abigail," Sarah had said.

"Not like this."

145

"What about Lord Ivo's escape from debtor's prison in *Too Lonely My Heart*?"

I just smiled. It was so great to be able to be friends with Sarah and the FBO club at the same time. I think it was the best week of my life. And even if I suddenly got bad breath just as I was saying hello to Denver James, the party would still be fun. For one thing, Pamela had invited Josh Baron. He hadn't said anything to me since that day in the cafeteria, but he did smile at me in homeroom on Wednesday, and on Thursday I found a green sour ball on my desk that I'm sure was from him. The FBO club were so excited when I told them about him. Kate is positive he's going to ask me to the Thanksgiving Dance, and if he does, Pam said I could borrow her black sweater with the sparkles on it.

Anyway, I was so excited, I woke up at about six o'clock in the morning. We were all supposed to meet at the train station at eleven-thirty. The real party started at three o'clock, but the FBO club and Sarah were invited early to meet the cast and have lunch. Pamela's mom was meeting us in New York, so we were going to take the train with Lucia. I was kind of glad about that, because, to tell you the truth, Pam's mom kind of scares me. She's always dressed up in these beautiful clothes, and she wears mink coats and perfume. My mom wears blue jeans and smells like barbeque sauce. This way, Lucia would sit on the other end of the train car and we could all sit together. It would be kind of like going all by ourselves.

But eleven-thirty was a long way away. It was barely light outside. I knew I couldn't sleep anymore, so I put on my slippers and bathrobe and went down to the living room. I figured that *Sesame Street* was probably on TV or something. I don't like to admit it, but I secretly still watch *Sesame Street* sometimes. Ernie cracks me up. I had just gotten myself a glass of milk and a bagel when I heard someone knocking really softly on the kitchen window. It was Sarah.

"Abigail?" she whispered through the glass.

"Sarah! It's six o'clock in the morning," I said as I opened the kitchen door. "What are you doing here?"

"I couldn't sleep, so I decided to take a walk. I saw the light on in your kitchen. What are you doing up so early?"

"I was so excited, I couldn't sleep, either. Do you want to come in?"

"Abigail, I must speak with you, it's terribly urgent, I've been simply fraught with anxiety," Sarah said as she came in the door.

"What's up?" I asked.

Sarah didn't seem like her usual self. She sat down at the kitchen table and put her head in her hands and sighed.

"Abigail, I cannot possibly attend this party

today. I thought I could. I really tried. But I know now that it would be an utter disaster," she said. "Please send my sincere apologies to Pamela. I certainly wouldn't want to insult her just as we are becoming better acquainted."

"Sarah, what are you talking about?" I asked. "You have to come to the party. It won't be any fun at all without you."

I couldn't believe she was saying this. Just as everything was finally going great, and the FBO club and Sarah were getting to be friends, and we were all going to meet Denver James. Why would Sarah want to ruin everything?

"Why can't you come?" I asked.

"Well, I'm cursed. You know, like Lady Olivia de Montebello in *The Ruby of Love*."

"*What?*" I said. "Sarah, you're crazy."

"Abigail, every party I've ever attended has resulted in disaster. When I was seven, I fell right into a hive of yellow jackets at Nancy Rivers's picnic, and everyone got stung and had to be rushed to the hospital. When I was nine, I gave my cousin Alison a piece of chocolate at her brother's bar mitzvah."

"So what was wrong with that?" I asked.

"She's allergic to chocolate, Abigail. She threw up on the rabbi," Sarah said.

"Oh."

"Once, a birthday party I was attending had to

be canceled because of a hurricane. Shall I go on?" Sarah asked.

I didn't know what to say. It *did* sound as if Sarah had some pretty bad luck at parties, but I couldn't believe she was really cursed. Actually, I thought she was just covering up for something else. There was some reason why she didn't want to come to the party. But I wasn't sure what it was.

"Well, I don't believe in curses, Sarah. But if you don't come to Pam's party, I'll be so angry at you that I'll find someone to really put a curse on you. What do you think of that?" I said. But I smiled when I said it, because I didn't want her to think I would really put a curse on her or anything like that.

"Abigail, don't be angry at me. I just can't possibly go."

"But why, Sarah? Really, why?" I asked.

"Oh, Abigail . . . just look at me!"

I looked. She was wearing plaid flannel pajamas and a big floppy sweater that probably belonged to her brother, and those slipper-sock things that Granny Gargul always gives Paul for Christmas. She didn't look too great. But most people don't in their pajamas.

"What's wrong with you?" I asked.

"Oh, I look terrible. I never have the right thing to wear. My hair is dreadful, and look, I have this space between my front teeth. How can I go to the most important party of the year?" Sarah said. "Is that a bagel?"

"Yes. Do you want one?"

"If you please, Abigail. I think I would find it comforting."

I cut open a bagel and started to put cream cheese on it.

"Sarah, I would be happy to help you get ready for the party," I said, handing her the bagel.

"What could you do? You'd have to shave my head and give me braces."

I could see that the bagel wasn't helping, so I made her a glass of chocolate milk.

"Sarah, all you have to do is fix your hair up and maybe wear some clothes that don't droop so much. You know, you'd really be very pretty if you tried."

"Do you think so?" Sarah said. "Do you think I could be as pretty as you are?"

I practically choked on my bagel. I couldn't believe that Sarah thought I was so much prettier than her. I don't think I'm very pretty at all, but it sure made me feel good when she said that.

"Prettier." I was looking right at her when I said it, and I really meant it. Sarah has beautiful eyes and nice skin and a great smile, even with the space. So what if her hair is a little wild?

"C'mon," I said. "We'll make you the prettiest girl at the party."

Sarah started whooping.

"What's so funny?" I asked.

"Abigail," Sarah said between whoops. "You're the best friend I ever had. But this is *Pam's* party, remember?"

"All right. Second prettiest," I said. "C'mon."

We spent the rest of the morning getting ready. First, I braided all Sarah's hair into a French braid the way Pamela had taught me. Then we found a great outfit for her to wear. She had these black jeans that she never wore to school because they were too tight. She thought they made her look too skinny. I wish that was my problem. Then we found this gorgeous, romantic, lacy blouse that her mother got in Mexico. I lent her the gold hoop earrings that my father sent me for my birthday, since they never looked that good on me anyway. They looked perfect on Sarah. Her mother even let her wear a little blush, because it was a special occasion. When we were all done, she looked fantastic. Sarah was so excited, she gave me a big hug. "Oh, Abigail, I feel like Cinderella. And you're my fairy godmother."

"You see," I said. "It's going to be a great party."

"Yes. Now let's just hope I don't set something on fire."

The FBO club couldn't believe it when we showed up at the train station. They all came running up to Sarah, telling her how pretty she looked. Sarah just smiled and smiled. Even with Pamela there, Sarah sort of stole the show. Not that Pamela didn't look gorgeous, as usual, in her royal-blue sweater with the lace collar, and her hair all tied up in a big velvet bow in back. But everyone expects Pam to look great. Sarah was a big surprise. I wasn't jealous, though, the way I sometimes am of Pam. I was just happy for Sarah. The party was off to a great start.

Then, while we were on the train, another amazing thing happened. Beth was telling us all about the play, and doing imitations of Ms. Orpen, the music teacher. Sarah was whooping and whooping, which was making everyone else laugh harder. Then, suddenly, she stopped laughing and hit me really really hard on the arm.

"Abigail," she said. "Don't turn around."

So, of course, I instantly turned around.

"Oh, my gosh!" I said.

"What is it?" Pam asked, trying to see behind me.

It was Al. Al the museum guard. He was sitting two seats behind me on the train, reading a magazine.

"I'm going to say 'Hi,' " Sarah said.

She got up from her seat and walked right over to him. He was as cute as ever. The FBO club all stared at her, and at him, with their mouths hanging open.

"Who is he?" Beth whispered to me.

So while Sarah chatted with Al as if she had known him all her life, I told them the story of Al the museum guard.

"Wow," said Pam. "I may start hanging around museums."

I was so proud of Sarah, I could hardly stand it. I never could have talked to him in a million years. When she got back to our seat, he looked over at us all and waved, which made Kate and Beth giggle like crazy.

"What did you say to him?" Pamela asked breathlessly.

"I just told him how much we enjoyed the costume exhibit, and thanked him for showing us around. He didn't remember me until I reminded him," Sarah said. "He asked me if we wanted to come back some day and see the Egyptian wing. That's where he works. And, oh, Abigail, his name *is* Alexander."

The FBO club all started talking at once. They were so impressed with Sarah's bravery. Pam said she was *so* glad Sarah was her friend, and she wanted to plan a date to go to the museum as soon as possible. That was certainly a change from the old Pam. And then Sarah and I started to tell them about the Alexander in our book, about him being a disguised Italian prince, and about the evil marquis and Annabella and the ball and everything.

They were totally into it. In fact, they didn't even notice when we pulled into the station until Lucia came and got us.

"That's such a wonderful story, Sarah," Beth said.

"It's so romantic," said Kate.

"It's as good as *Your Life to Lead*," said Pam. "I'm sorry I ever made fun of your writing, Sarah. I think you're a very good writer."

That was the nicest thing that Pam could have said. It made me so happy, I could hardly breathe.

In the taxi on the way to the party, everyone was talking and laughing, and planning what to say to Denver James. It was just like the old days wth the FBO club, only better, because now Sarah was there.

The most fun thing, though, was when we got to the set. On TV it looks like there really is a town called Oak River, where the show is filmed, but when you go to the TV studio, you can see that it's all fake. We walked through all the houses. The little cottage by the lake, where Denver and Monica first fell in love, has a door that goes right into the great front hall of the Porter mansion. It's weird, but fun. We got to go all over the set and sit on the furniture and look through the cameras. Then Pam's mother came and led us into the living room of the Hanovers' house where she had set up lunch for us.

"This is the most extraordinary and wonderful

place," Sarah said. "I feel like I'm dreaming."

She took a big bite out of a roast beef sandwich. Just at that moment, Denver James walked in the door. Kate sort of gasped. Beth sort of choked. I sort of sneezed. Sarah swallowed really fast and turned a little red in the face. Pamela just smiled.

"I hear there's a birthday party going on here," he said. "I just wanted to wish you a very happy one."

He walked right over to Pam and gave her a little kiss on the cheek. He was much shorter in person than I thought he would be, and he looked a little older than I thought, too. But he was *sooooo* gorgeous and nice. He said hello and shook all of our hands. Mine didn't even sweat at all. And he even said we were the prettiest bunch of girls he'd ever seen. Which was a total lie, because every girl on the whole show is perfect-looking, but it was nice of him to say it anyway.

Then the guy who plays Harold, Mr. Porter's butler, came over and said "hi," too, and told Pam that her mother was "absolutely a fantastic human being." Pam didn't know what to say to that at all. It's a pretty strange thing to be told about your own mother.

"Well, Dave old boy, I think we should be going. Have a fun party, girls," Harold the butler said.

They waved at us and walked out.

"Why did Harold call him 'Dave'?" Kate asked Pamela.

I had to admit I had been wondering the same thing myself.

"That's his real name. Dave Connor," Pam said.

"How dreadfully disappointing," Sarah said.

I was sort of disappointed, too. Dave Connor. It just didn't have much of a ring to it.

"I guess I never thought about him having a real name," Kate said.

"Dave," Beth said. "It's so . . ."

"Ordinary?" I said.

"Yeah," Beth said.

We sat for a while and thought about Denver James being named Dave. It was a little depressing.

"He is terribly handsome, though," Sarah said. "I don't suppose he can help being named Dave."

That made everyone cheer up a little.

"And he did kiss you on the cheek, Pam!" Beth said. "It was just fantastic!"

After that, everyone started talking at once. He was so handsome, he was so nice, he said we were the prettiest bunch of girls he'd ever seen. We couldn't believe it had really happened. We met Denver James! It was a truly great day.

"Okay, it's present time!" said Pam when we had talked ourselves out.

"Pamela!" her mother said, coming into the room with a huge plate of cookies. "That's not very polite."

"It's okay, Mrs. Baldwin," Kate said. "We want

to give Pam our presents." She pulled a box out of the bag she had been carrying. "Open mine first, Pam," she said.

Pam opened it. It was a pair of fancy barrettes with little pearls all over them.

"Oh, Katie, they're beautiful," Pam said.

"Now me," said Beth.

Beth had gotten Pam a tape of her favorite group. I had gotten her a pair of dangling earrings shaped like little starfish. Pam loved all of the gifts. Then it was Sarah's turn.

"I hope you like it, Pamela," Sarah said a little nervously.

I could understand why she might be worried. She didn't know Pam very well, after all. And the two of them were kind of different.

"I'm sure I will," said Pam.

It was a little package wrapped in beautiful flowered paper. Pam opened it up. Inside was a book, covered in fabric with roses all over it. It had a tiny little lock on it, and a key to the lock.

"I know you like to write, Pamela. I thought you might like a special book to write in," Sarah said.

Pam just looked at it for a minute. I was very worried. It seemed like a present that Sarah would like, not Pamela. But then Pamela smiled a really big smile. "Oh, Sarah, it's exactly what I wanted."

"It is?" asked Kate.

"You're not a writer, Kate, so you wouldn't understand," Pam said.

"Happy Birthday," Sarah said.

Pamela smiled again. "Now I have something for all of you." She pulled a shopping bag out from under the table. It was full of beautifully wrapped boxes, with big pink ribbons on them. Pam started to hand them out to all of us, first to me, and then to Kate and Beth. It made me feel good to get a present from Pam, but I felt bad that Sarah was being left out. Then Pam pulled out one more box and handed it to Sarah!

"This one is for you, Sarah, if you want it," Pam said. "It's a special present just for club members."

"But I thought your club was For Blondes Only," Sarah said. "I'm not a blonde."

"Well, obviously, Sarah, I can see that," Pam replied. "But I think we can fix that problem."

Sarah looked at me a little nervously. I think she was worried that Pam might want to dye her hair blonde or something.

"Go on, open them," Pam said.

So we all ripped the paper off our boxes and opened them up. Inside each was a T-shirt in a beautiful shade of pink. And in blue writing on each one were the words "*Not* For Blondes Only."

"Oh, Pam, it's beautiful," Sarah cried. "I would be honored to wear it."

"Really, Sarah?" Pam said. "I was afraid that maybe, after everything that's happened, you wouldn't."

"*Au contraire*," Sarah said. "For as Lord Ivo often says, 'the seeds of great affection are often born in adversity.' "

Everyone nodded when she said that, but I don't think any of us had a clue what it meant.

"I'm terribly proud," Sarah went on, "to be, well, to be . . . *not* a blonde."

Everyone clapped, and Pam went over and gave Sarah a little squeeze. I felt totally happy.

"You see?" I whispered to Sarah. "Everything's been great! Aren't you glad you came?"

"Oh, Abigail," Sarah said, starting to pull the shirt over her head, "this is the best day of my life!"

Just then Pam's mother walked in, carrying the cake and singing "Happy Birthday to You." We all joined in, except Sarah, who had somehow gotten her arm stuck in the T-shirt. Just as Pam's mother walked over to the table, Sarah's arm came popping out of the shirt. It hit Pam's mother, and the cake went flying up in the air and landed right on Pamela's good black shoes.

"Oh, dear," Sarah said. "Oh, Abigail, I told you I was cursed."

Pam looked at her shoes for a minute. Then she looked at Sarah, who was turning bright red from embarrassment. Then she started to laugh. Just a little giggle at first, but soon Beth joined in, and then Kate, and then me. And, finally, after a little while, I heard, "Whoop, whoop, whoop." And then Pam said, "Welcome to the club, Sarah."

What happens when Kate gets the lead in the school play instead of Beth, and Sarah is a rock-and-roll D.J. for a day? Read the second *Not For Blondes Only* book, SHOW TIME!

About the Authors

Betsy Lifton and Karen Lifton have been sisters since birth. They have been writing as a team for many years, though the *Not* For Blondes Only books are their first novels. Betsy lives in Westchester County, New York, with her husband, son, and daughter. Karen lives in Buffalo, New York, with her husband and daughter. They are both brunette.

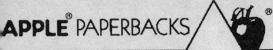

THE BABY·SITTERS CLUB®

Collect Them All!

by Ann M. Martin

The seven girls at Stoneybrook Middle School get into all kinds
of adventures...with school, boys, and, of course, baby-sitting!